DEAD

Coming soon by David Gatward:

Book 2 of THE DEAD: The Dark
Book 3 of THE DEAD: The Damned

For more information visit:
www.davidgatward.com

THE DEAD

DAVID GATWARD

*Hodder
Children's
Books*

A division of Hachette Children's Books

First published in Great Britain in 2010
by Hodder Children's Books

1

A Catalogue record for this book is available from the British Library

ISBN 978 0 340 99969 1

Typeset in Caslon by Avon DataSet Ltd,
Bidford-on-Avon, Warwickshire

Printed and bound in Great Britain by
Bookmarque Ltd, Croydon, Surrey

The paper and board used in this paperback by Hodder Children's Books are
natural recyclable products made from wood grown in sustainable forests.
The manufacturing processes conform to the environmental regulations
of the country of origin.

Hodder Children's Books
A division of Hachette Children's Books
338 Euston Road, London NW1 3BH
An Hachette UK company
www.hachette.co.uk

For Su – for putting up with the dream
and being part of the reality

'Pity is for the living, envy is for the Dead . . .'

Mark Twain

1
🕱 ROTTING MEAT 🕱

It was when Lazarus opened his bedroom door that he noticed the smell.

'What the hell's that?'

He'd been on the phone for the past half hour to Craig – best mate and wannabe best-selling novelist – and was in serious need of a slash. It was late night, early morning. Two o'clock was coming round quickly. Lazarus hadn't yet bothered to get undressed and his black jeans and black T-shirt made him look like a shadow gone walkabout. With school now over for the summer, he wasn't too fussed about getting much sleep. And anyway, he liked the night; always had. Darkness felt comforting, the midnight hours always a quiet break from life, particularly the school days he hated.

'What's up?' asked Craig.

'A stink in the house,' said Lazarus. 'It reeks like rotting meat!'

For a second he just stood there, holding his left hand up to his nose, the phone in his right against his ear. He chanced another sniff. It was rank.

'Smells like the kitchen bin after a month in the sun,' he said. 'But I'm sure I emptied it this morning.'

'You doing domestic chores?' said Craig. 'I'm amazed!'

'I'm home alone, mate,' said Lazarus into his mobile. 'The au pair's gone.'

'You're kidding me!'

'Seriously,' said Lazarus, unable to hide the happiness in his voice. 'Just upped and left. Found a note on the kitchen table telling me to call the agency for a replacement – as if!'

Lazarus edged forward into the hallway. The bathroom was at the other end of the hall and he was getting desperate.

As he walked on, the only sound in the house other than his sockless shuffle was the faint ticking of the many old clocks his dad collected. He hated the sound – his dad seemed to care more for them than he did him.

When he wasn't working, he was fiddling with the things, tinkering here and there. He certainly spent more time with them than with Lazarus, polishing them and making sure their timing was right, that they were wound up just so. Lazarus just didn't get what his dad saw in them. They were just clocks after all. Why couldn't he be interested in something decent, like cars? Clocks were just sad and a little pathetic. Lazarus fancied taking a sledgehammer to the whole damned lot of them.

'Can't believe she left you,' said Craig. 'You think this is how it's going to be with you and women from now on?'

'Ha ha,' said Lazarus, dead pan.

'She give any reasons?'

'Some crap about missing her boyfriend and needing to see the world,' said Lazarus, finally reaching the bathroom. 'You know, the usual blah-blah-blah emotional stuff. Just a minute . . .'

Lazarus put the phone down and thirty seconds later pulled the flush.

'Much better,' he said, picking up the phone again after washing his hands.

'I heard everything,' said Craig. 'Thanks. No, really.'

Lazarus laughed and headed back to his room.

'What about your dad?' asked Craig. 'Does he know about the au pair?'

'Hasn't a clue,' said Lazarus, a smile creeping across his face. 'Result or what?'

'You lucky sod,' said Craig. 'When's he back?'

'No idea, just said he was away on business and left me with the usual: a firm handshake and enough money to buy takeaway for a month.'

'Nice.'

'Oh, it was emotional. Always is. You know Dad.'

Craig laughed. 'Wasn't she due to leave anyway?'

'Yeah,' said Lazarus, 'but not till after my birthday. And that's still two weeks off.'

'Oh yes, the big sixteen,' said Craig, his voice an attempt at sounding mysterious. 'Old enough to join the army, become a dad, but not drive a car; where's the logic? How's the weird smell?'

'Gone,' said Lazarus. 'How freaky is that?'

'Not very,' said Craig. 'Now your dad being generous – that's weird.'

Lazarus, now back in his bedroom, lay down on his bed.

He knew what Craig was getting at. Dad never made much of birthdays, of anything really. His life was his work, though how being a locksmith and security consultant could be so interesting utterly baffled Lazarus. But this birthday was going to be different, apparently.

A year ago, they'd made an agreement: he'd clean up his act at school and his dad would give him something on his sixteenth that would change his life. The thought made Lazarus laugh, but not in a good way. What the hell was there his dad could ever give him that would do that?

He still hadn't any idea as to what this something was. His dad had given no clues. Not a hint, nothing. The only thing his dad had ever given him of value was a small silver key on a thick silver neck chain on his thirteenth. It was for good luck, apparently. Well, it hadn't brought him any, had it? Except for a bit of attention from girls, who thought it looked cool and always commented on it. That was something at least. So he always wore it. But as far as jewellery was concerned that was where it started and stopped.

Craig came back with, 'You reckon the deal with your dad still holds?'

'I've held up my end of the bargain,' said Lazarus, his voice hard. 'He'd better hold up his.'

'True,' said Craig. 'You're Mr Clean at school now.'

Lazarus had never liked school. He found lessons both easy and boring and the rules and restrictions pointless and suffocating. He didn't break the rules on purpose, it was – in his mind at least – just something he had no control over. Like when he'd refused to cut his blond hair for eighteen months, then hacked it off short and ragged himself late one night. And dyed it black. He still wore it the same way: unruly, uneven and gelled to hell.

As everyone else struggled with quadratic equations, European history and biology, Lazarus sailed through. It irritated those around him, frustrated his teachers, disappointed his dad, sent himself crazy.

Detention was a weekly occurrence, but he'd never been expelled, and that was for two reasons. One, he'd always had the sense to make sure that any of the trouble he caused never went too far. What was the point of burning the school down, when it was so much more fun to break in now and again and write far too accurate limericks about the head of maths on the display boards in the classrooms? And two, he aced everything. Well, everything except for the exams he'd not been arsed to sit.

Lazarus sank back into the pillows on his bed and stretched out. The house, large and silent, was now his castle. He smiled to himself in the knowledge that he could pretty much do what he wanted till his dad came home. Like go get a snack at two a.m. Brilliant.

He sat up and swung his legs off the bed as Craig came back with a question about what his plans were for the summer.

'No idea,' Lazarus said. 'Can't do much till Dad's back anyway. What about you?'

'Funny you should ask,' said Craig.

'I didn't,' smiled Lazarus. 'You did.'

Craig said, 'How do you fancy going away for a few days? Down to my parents' caravan? It's not exactly posh, but ... Anyway, they've decided I'm old enough to go on my own if I want to, but only if someone goes with me.'

Lazarus grinned. 'You need someone to tuck you in at night?'

'No,' said Craig. 'I need someone who looks old enough to get served at the bar.'

The idea of going away for a few days to piss around in a caravan with Craig was brilliant. 'It'll have to be after Dad's back,' said Lazarus. 'That OK?'

'Totally,' said Craig. 'Now about that movie I lent you. Did you watch it tonight? What did you think? Did you like it? Or was it simply too complex for your tiny brain?'

Lazarus went to answer, but as he stood up to head off on a snack-finding mission, his head suddenly swam and his vision went fuzzy. Then he toppled forward on to his knees, almost cracking his head open on his desk.

And he just knew he was about to throw up.

2

BURNED WOOD

Lazarus retched:

'What's up?' asked Craig, hearing Lazarus groan and sounding almost concerned. 'You been at your dad's drinks cabinet again?'

Lazarus didn't answer. Instead he leant forward, bracing himself against the floor with his hands, focusing his mind on not being sick, forcing his stomach to keep its contents, swallowing. Bile burned in his throat and that horribly familiar metallic taste was round his mouth, like the sensation of sticking his tongue on a battery to check it was live. It was a stupid phobia, he knew (and that was why no one knew about it), but being sick really did freak the hell out of him.

'Lazarus? What's up?'

But Lazarus wasn't listening – he was concentrating on

not being reintroduced to the contents of his stomach.

He slowly reached a hand up on to his desk. Shaking his head to clear it, he opened and closed his eyes, rubbed them. White stars burst behind his eyelids and his stomach flipped. Then a strange piercing sound inside his skull made him wince and his ears popped. It reminded him of the one and only time he'd ever been on a plane – the sensation as it had climbed into the sky. But why it was happening now in the middle of the night he'd no idea. Maybe he'd stood up too fast. Yeah, that must be it. But God he felt awful.

Eventually, the feeling subsided. Lazarus pushed himself up from his desk, opened his eyes and looked out through his window. It was a black night, winter-dark despite it being July, and clear, the moon like a smudge of chalk on a blackboard. And it was cold. The summer had been a total washout since a few hot days in May. The gardens around the house were all in shadow, staring out over an old, sleepy Somerset skyline laced with trees and new-build houses attempting to blend in.

'Lazarus? Are you OK? What's up? You haven't gone and died on me, have you?'

'Yeah, sorry mate,' said Lazarus. 'Stood up too fast I think.'

'Sounded like you fell over.'

'That's because I did,' said Lazarus. 'My head went all weird and I thought I was going to throw. What were you saying?'

'The movie,' said Craig. 'You loved it, right?'

'Oh that,' said Lazarus, his head still a bit groggy, thinking back to what he'd just finished watching. 'Your recommendations suck.'

'It's a classic!' said Craig, his voice all mock shock and despair. 'Director's a genius. You've got no taste.'

'Guess not,' said Lazarus and walked across to his bedroom door. His head was clear now, and a snack was definitely necessary. 'For some reason, badly dubbed seventies Italian horror goes right over my head. What have you been up to, or do I not need to ask?'

Lazarus knew Craig was smiling.

'Watching *Most Haunted*!' said Craig. 'Best-of DVD.'

'You just fancy the woman who fronts it.'

'Ha ha,' said Craig. 'And I've been writing again. Just finished this amazing book about how adults go nuts and start killing anyone younger than nineteen; awesome stuff! Really inspired me.'

'You're ill,' said Lazarus. 'So what are you getting me for my birthday?'

He dreaded the answer; Craig had a reputation for buying him useless crap. Last year he'd trumped everything: Lazarus still hadn't found a place to put the wicker pig. Apparently Craig had looked for a wicker man – some pointless horror movie reference – but only found a pig.

Craig said, 'A personality and taste. You on the move?'

'Yeah,' said Lazarus. 'Food to the rescue of a dodgy stomach.'

'Good call,' said Craig. 'I'll join you.'

Phone to his ear, Lazarus strolled back over to his bedroom door and pulled it open. He sniffed the air. 'That smell's totally gone.'

'You sure it wasn't just a fart?' said Craig. 'Your guts are always rotten. I blame all that mouldy cheese you eat.'

'It's blue cheese, you tit,' said Lazarus.

Lazarus didn't say any more, but he was a bit confused. He hadn't a clue what the smell was or where it had come from. He wondered if a refuse truck had gone past, but it was too early for anyone to be out doing the bins.

He walked on. To his left, the landing gave way to the stairs. At the top of these was the main bedroom – his dad's – occupied by nothing but practical furniture, neat clothes and pictures of his mum. The stairs themselves turned a hundred and eighty degrees in a large, oak sweep to the hall on the ground floor.

Lazarus walked down the first flight on to the small landing halfway between the floors. Moonlight glanced through a towering stained-glass window above it, casting a blurred smear of colour from the glass down the stairs like spilled paint. By the time he stepped forward to make his way down to the ground floor, the smell had totally gone.

At the bottom of the stairs, his feet feeling the cold of the old quarry tiles that covered the hallway floor, Lazarus stood for a moment in the darkness, sniffing the air just to make sure. No, there was no trace of any stench. It wasn't coming from his right, which led off and round past the downstairs toilet and his dad's study. Neither was it coming from the left, which led past the lounge.

With a shrug, he hung left, past the lounge door,

through the dining room and in to the kitchen.

'Well?' said Craig. 'What was it?'

'No idea,' said Lazarus, reaching out to open the fridge. The light lit up the kitchen and made the night on the other side of the window above the sink seem all the darker. He could hear Craig sorting himself out some food. 'What are you having?'

'Fish-finger sandwich,' said Craig. 'Gastronomic heaven! You?'

'Cheese on toast,' said Lazarus. 'With Marmite.'

A few moments later, the cheese was under the grill then on a plate. Lazarus left the fridge door open, preferring the light it cast to that of the main one in the ceiling above. It made the night seem more immediate.

The toast was soon gone and the kitchen again plunged into darkness. Lazarus could now see clearly through the windows without the reflecting light from the fridge. The garden out back was still. The tree that grew at the edge of the worn brick path seemed to lean under the weight of the moonlight on its leaves, but unlike Lazarus, wasn't suffering from all the cloud and rain. If anything, the world looked greener, he thought, but was it really too much to ask for a summer to at least drip a little bit of sunshine into the day now and again?

Lazarus walked through to the dining room. He caught the faint image of his reflection in a mirror on the wall. On his right arm, just below his T-shirt, the mark he'd had since he was a baby stared back. It was a burn, with ragged, torn edges. It was the only scar he'd got from the car accident, the one that had killed the mum he couldn't even remember.

He quickly pushed away any thoughts about the woman his dad had fallen in love with all those years ago. He'd never known her. She was gone, dead. And there wasn't any coming back, he knew that for sure. She was just a face in photos in his dad's bedroom and around the house. Photos his dad made sure, almost religiously, were utterly free of dust.

'Time to hit the sack,' said Lazarus. 'You around tomorrow? Fancy doing a DVD-athon?'

'Totally,' said Craig. 'But only if I get to choose the movies. Your taste sucks.'

Lazarus heard Craig yawn. He was about to say *See you tomorrow*, when, from directly ahead of him, the smell came again, driven by a gust that came out of nowhere and disappeared just as quickly.

He coughed, gagged, nearly threw up. Then just like before, his head spun, his ears popped, but he managed to steady himself before he hit the deck, reaching out for the wall. The sensation made him groan, and for a second he thought he was going to pass out.

'Now what?'

'It's that smell again,' said Lazarus, shaking his head. 'It's come back. It's unbelievable!'

'Rats,' said Craig. 'Can't be anything else. I'd put your shoes on if I were you; the little sods'll have your toes.'

'Can't be rats,' said Lazarus, walking back into the hall. 'I'd have heard them or noticed them or something before now, wouldn't I?'

The smell was getting stronger and he was finding it a real struggle to breathe. His hand firmly clamped over his mouth and nose, he looked down the hall and saw something that hadn't been there when he'd come down the stairs earlier on. And it made him stop dead. A faint red glow was licking out into the hall from under the lounge door, like it was trying to taste the tiles.

Perhaps he'd left the television on? It certainly wasn't a fire – one hadn't been lit since back in February. But that's what it looked like. And that was impossible.

'It's coming from the lounge,' he said at last, his eyes fixed on the strange glow, his feet refusing to move. 'And I know this is going to sound totally nuts, but there's a red light coming from under the door, like the fire's been lit.'

'A fire?' said Craig. 'I know the summer's been a pile of arse, but I didn't realise you were such a wuss. I bet you've got a hot water bottle too, haven't you?'

But Lazarus didn't laugh. With the smell again and now the weird red light, he was having trouble not just freaking out on the spot.

Edging forward, he kept staring at the red light. It had to be the television. It just had to be. It couldn't be anything else . . .

He reached out for the door handle, twisting it left, then right, then left again. It was always stiff and took a few goes to open. This time though it was taking longer than usual, and he thought about his dad and how he spent more time with his clocks than doing something useful like the occasional fix-up job round the house.

Eventually the handle clicked and the door eased open, whispering across a well-worn arc in the carpet on the floor on the other side.

The smell and the heat took Lazarus's breath away. He stumbled backwards, coughing.

'Mate, what's going on?' said Craig, and this time he actually sounded concerned. 'Is it rats?'

'I ... don't know ...' Lazarus replied, and walked into the room.

The curtains were drawn, the darkness warm. An orange-red glow burned the walls from a fire roaring in the grate. The air had a tang of burned wood. But it was also filled with the reek that was almost making his eyes bleed.

'So what was it?' asked Craig. 'TV?'

Lazarus was staring at the fire, couldn't pull his eyes away from it, knew he hadn't lit it.

'Listen mate,' he said, his words drying in his throat, his brain close to short-circuiting, 'I'll call you back, OK?'

He cut the call before he had a chance to hear Craig's reply. Then, as he slowly lowered the phone from his ear, he looked away from the fireplace, allowing his eyes to adjust to the reddish darkness in the room. Soon, things took shape: the sideboard, television, sofa, piano. It all looked very normal.

All, that was, except for the dark shadow, sitting in the wooden rocking chair closest to the fire, which turned to face him.

3
🕱 BLOODY WOUNDS 🕱

L azarus screamed.

Not like a girl. Not like a child. But like someone who had come face to face with something that demanded a scream as the only possible response.

The figure's body was bathed in firelight, the rocking chair horribly still. Its head was bald, the skin ripped away in strips and in places Lazarus, horrified and scared beyond anything he'd ever experienced in his life before, could see the milky glow of bone. Its ears were gone, nothing more than stumps that looked like melted candles. The face was a mass of tears and cuts, slicing across it this way and that, the nose severed in half. The mouth had no lips; just great, bloody wounds where they looked like they had been torn off. Its teeth reflected the fire.

The phone clattered from Lazarus's nerveless fingers.

He pulled his eyes away, stumbled backwards, slammed into the wall, knocked his head. He turned to the lounge door, the only exit, to see the door slowly click shut. He tried to move, force his legs to drag him towards it, but his body refused to shift. Then he looked back to the thing in the lounge and found he couldn't draw his eyes away this time, no matter how much he wanted to.

Lazarus couldn't yet tell if the thing was male or female, but it was definitely naked, or so he guessed. He couldn't see any clothes, not unless they, like the rest of its body, were covered – no, *drenched* – in blood. From there on down, the figure was stripped of most of its skin. He could see individual muscles and tendons tensing, relaxing. And around the figure's feet, as they rested together on the floor, a dark pool was spreading.

But as Lazarus stared, it seemed that the thing was healing itself. He could see new skin forming, creeping fresh and pink across exposed wounded flesh and muscle, covering up veins and arteries, stemming the flow of blood. It was a slow process, but it was definitely happening. With hideous fascination, he stared as the body took form in front of him.

Lazarus's skin was clammy and his heart was battering at his ribs; he was seconds away from throwing up. He didn't give a chuff who or what this was in his house – he just wanted to get the hell out, and fast.

'I'm sorry I frightened you,' said the figure.

To Lazarus the voice sounded hollow, like an echo in a tunnel, but it was definitely male.

'I had to come now, before it's too late.'

'Too late for what?' said Lazarus, ready to bolt. 'Who are you? What the hell happened to you?'

He couldn't stop staring. Whoever this was, his body was a total wreck. How was he even still alive?

'Hell happened to me,' said the man, and his face broke into a horrible grin, like a frozen death mask.

'Hell? What are you talking about?'

Lazarus was beyond terrified now. He didn't even know why he was talking, why he was asking questions.

'Oh, I'm sure you've heard of it,' said the man. 'Only forget all that myth about the devil and pits of fire. That's got nothing on the reality of the place. Trust me.'

Looking at him, that was the last thing Lazarus thought he would ever do. But he couldn't help thinking that whoever he was and wherever he was from, he sounded like he knew exactly what he was talking about.

Lazarus asked, 'How did you get in? I'll call the police!'

The man made a sound like a laugh. It rattled like grit in a tin.

'What do you know of death, Lazarus?'

The question hit Lazarus hard. He felt dazed by it, and angry. 'My mum was killed in a car accident,' he said, spitting each word. 'That's what I know about it. It's the end. And there ain't no coming back.' He could feel the anger getting the better of him, but he did his best to maintain some control. 'So why don't you just get the hell out of here and leave me alone? What are you – some kind of self-harming freak who likes to turn up in people's houses and scare them into believing in an afterlife? In God?'

The man laughed again. Only this time, much louder. 'No,' he said. 'I don't need to scare anyone to believe it. They believe it when they see it. All of them do. Now, tell me – where is your father?'

Dad? thought Lazarus. *What the* . . . 'What's he got to do with this?'

'Everything,' said the man. He stood up so quickly that Lazarus gasped. Every movement of his body was sharp and jagged, like his bones kept seizing up. 'Where is he?'

'Away on business,' said Lazarus.

Suddenly he felt all the more afraid; he'd just let on that he was home alone. What would this nutter do now, knowing that no one else was in the house?

'Really ...'

Lazarus heard the disbelief in the visitor's voice. The man bent over, grabbed a log and threw it on the fire. Smoke and flame burst from the fireplace, scorching the darkened room. A yellow-hot ember shot from the grate and landed on the carpet. Lazarus watched as the man leant forward and crushed it between his fingers, flicking the ash off into the fireplace. He then reached up with his left hand and wiped away a drop of blood from beneath his right eye. Fresh skin lay under the blood, covering up a section of his face. But those lips were still raw, completely ruined.

'I shall not harm you,' said the man, 'but I have no time for pleasantries. Your father, Lazarus. I must speak with him.'

Lazarus was horrified – he was sure he'd never said his name, not once. 'How do you know my name?'

The man just stared at Lazarus, rubbing his red, sticky hands together over the flames. The fire spat as the drops of blood from his hands fell into it. He leant his head forward, almost like he was praying, then he looked up at himself in the flickering reflection of the large, gilt mirror that hung above the fireplace. Lazarus could see a large bloody stain on the rocking chair.

'I know everyone's name,' said the man. Lazarus heard menace behind those words. 'If it helps, I will tell you mine. I am Red. It is such a beautiful colour, don't you think?'

'I don't care,' said Lazarus, and he could hear himself choking up. God, he was scared . . . terrified . . . 'Whatever your name is, just get out! Leave me alone!'

'If you father is not here,' said Red, ignoring Lazarus, 'then you will have to give him a message for me. I cannot wait and I cannot risk returning. As you can see from the way I look, I suffered enough for it just this once. And it took me two attempts to push through. Will you do that for me, Lazarus?'

Lazarus tried to gain some comfort from the sensation of the cold wall against his back, colder now thanks to his sweat freely running down it. What did Red mean by *two attempts to push through?* Lazarus remembered that stench and the nausea he'd felt – was all that to do with Red? But how? And was Red really saying he'd suffered all those injuries trying to visit his dad?

Instead of moving to leave, Red looked up at the mirror. With the index finger of his left hand, he drew two circles, a small one inside one much larger, like a fat ring doughnut. He placed a finger outside the lines, left a bloody dot. 'This is your world, Lazarus. Where we are right now. But this . . .' he pointed inside the first circle, 'this is the land of the Dead.'

Lazarus could taste tears now. This Red bloke was clearly insane. Land of the Dead? That was the stuff of horror movies, the kind of junk Craig would go nuts for.

Red still wasn't leaving. Lazarus was really beginning to fear for his life. Why couldn't this happen when his dad was home? When he had some back-up?

Red pointed at the smaller circle, sitting inside the larger. 'And this,' he said, 'is Hell.'

Lazarus stared at the bloody, dripping lines etched on to the mirror. 'I don't understand what you're saying,' he said, 'or what this has to do with my dad. Why are you here? Why the *hell* are you here?'

Red pointed at the rings. 'These veils stop our worlds colliding,' he said. 'Now and then the Dead slip through.'

'You mean ghosts?'

'Sometimes,' said Red. 'But they're few and far between. Easy to find, easy to send back. The Dead aren't so simple.'

'You're still not making any sense,' said Lazarus, wiping his tears with the back of his hand. 'What's this got to do with Dad?'

Red started to smudge the outer circle. 'Think,' he said, 'what would happen if the veils started to fail. Can you imagine what it would be like? If the Dead could cross over easily? If Hell was set free? Because if the Dead break free, Lazarus, believe me – Hell is coming.'

'Why are you telling me this?' Lazarus shouted. 'I don't understand!'

Red stopped smudging the bloody lines and looked at Lazarus. 'Your father is the Keeper, Lazarus,' he said. 'He sends back the Dead when they slip through.'

4

☠☠☠ ROTTEN BREATH ☠☠☠

'Shut up!' yelled Lazarus, finally losing control. 'Please, just shut up, will you? Dad's in security! He advises on safes and alarms! He's the dullest person I know! Hell? The Dead? What do you take me for? If you're here to murder me, then give it your best shot, but please just stop talking such total crap!'

Lazarus pushed himself away from the wall, bunched his fists. At that minute all he wanted to do was smash the freak hard in the face and destroy that horrible stare. Instead, he turned on his heels and bolted for the door. But when he grabbed the door handle, pain shot through his hand. He yanked it away. A circular burn was scorched into his palm. He could smell burning, like roast pork. It didn't hurt; it *killed*. The pain made him yell and he held his wrist with his other hand.

'I did not ask you to leave,' said Red, his voice the purr of a lion.

He was pointing at the door. Lazarus realised that the burn in his hand was Red's doing. He didn't know how – he just knew, and that in itself was scary enough.

Lazarus could feel panic building inside. He wasn't one for running away from trouble; he was used to being in the middle of it, often the cause. But here, facing Red, he felt trapped and desperate. This man wasn't a nutter, he was for real; and something about it all felt very, very wrong.

Red was at the mirror. Lazarus caught the reflection of his eyes. Then, without warning, he saw Red leap with frightening grace and speed from the fireplace and over the armchair. He landed silently and grabbed Lazarus, pinned him to the wall, his sweetly rotten breath making Lazarus want to puke, his shattered face almost touching Lazarus's own.

Red snatched at Lazarus's burned hand. Lazarus tried to pull away, but Red was ferociously strong; it felt like pulling at something welded to solid rock.

'Shush,' said Red. 'Shush . . .'

The sound carried through Red's naked teeth like the hiss of a rattlesnake, then his hand was on Lazarus's burn. Lazarus flinched as Red leaned in, his blood-wet skin glancing off Lazarus's cheek. The burning in his hand suddenly flared up, but as he screamed, the pain disappeared in an instant.

Red let go of Lazarus's hand and let it gently fall. He walked back to the fire.

Lazarus looked at his hand. The burn was gone, his hand completely healed.

'How—'

'Something is wrong, Lazarus,' said Red. 'Someone from your side is trying to make a hole in the veil. You cannot imagine how hard it is to fill that hole once it's dug. They have to be found! They have to be stopped! And your father is the only one with any chance of doing this!'

'Why would anyone do that?' asked Lazarus, his brain in full meltdown now.

'Pity,' said Red and Lazarus heard venom on his tongue. 'It was pity the last time, too. It is always pity. The living feeling sorry for the Dead, wanting to cross over, to help.'

'I can't listen to this any more,' said Lazarus. 'I can't—'

'You have to tell your father,' said Red. 'It's as if the Dead know someone is trying to come through from the land of the living. Don't you understand? The Dead are coming!'

'Ignoring the fact that you're talking total bull,' said Lazarus, still holding his hand, staring at it amazed, 'it's got nothing to do with me!'

'It's got everything to do with everyone,' said Red, taking a step towards him.

Lazarus could see bloody, torn footprints on the carpet. Strangely, he wondered how he was going to get them out before his dad came back.

'I'm not listening,' said Lazarus. He started to edge back towards the door. 'Whatever it is you think you're talking about, or trying to do, I'm not listening.'

'It cannot be allowed to happen again!' said Red.

At this, Lazarus stopped in his tracks. 'What do you mean, again?'

'When someone dies,' said Red, his voice quieter, his feet slipping damp smudges across the carpet, 'they cross the veil. At these points, if the Dead sense it quickly enough, they can slip back while the veil is still weak. And they do.'

'So how did you get through?'

'I am not one of the Dead,' said Red.

'Then what are you?' Lazarus shouted, having had more than enough of this insane conversation. 'A demon? That's all that's missing from this, isn't it? A big demon in your story to really scare me!'

Red roared. The sound forced Lazarus on to his knees, his hands clamped over his ears. It was as if Red's yell was trying to rip into every molecule in his body, tear them apart. Then Lazarus looked up. What he saw he knew would be burned into his mind for eternity.

He saw wings.

They exploded from Red's back, bursting out into the room, slamming into the lounge walls. They were beaten and battered and ripped and torn, bloody like crows' wings attacked by a cat. Impossibly large grey feathers, those that were more than just shredded remains, fluttered with every wing beat.

The right wing crashed through an old bookcase with glass doors, embedding itself into the brickwork behind.

Shattered glass fell like hail and the books were hewn into a thousand pieces. The left wing smashed a picture Lazarus had never really liked and scorched a black tear through the wall. Still on his knees, Lazarus ducked out of the way of flying debris, felt it sting him as it rained down.

'I am one of the Fallen,' said Red. 'That is all you need to know. For now.'

A new terror slammed into Lazarus. Was he on about angels now? But that was impossible, just the stuff of fantasies and fanatics . . .

He heard himself whimper, 'Don't kill me . . . please . . .' his voice breaking.

'Kill you?' said Red, and he was up close again, pulling Lazarus to his feet with ease and holding him round the neck against the wall. 'I'm trying to save you! Just tell your father what I have told you. He will know what to do. Understand?'

'No,' said Lazarus, his voice barely a whimper, hissing out over the soft squeeze of Red's hand on his neck. 'I don't understand any of this.'

'You need to think of the veil like a dam,' said Red, reaching out to tap the end of a bloody finger on Lazarus's forehead. 'Leaks are easy to deal with. But if someone goes and punches a hole in it, you not only get a flood, the whole thing can collapse.'

Lazarus let Red speak, had no choice anyway.

'I could let them win, you know that don't you?' said Red, his fingers slipping slowly from Lazarus's neck down across his shoulder, on to his arm. 'I could sit back and let them swarm and scorch the Earth.'

'Get off me,' coughed Lazarus, gulping to stop himself throwing up as well as grab some air.

Red's fingers were gentle, stroking almost. And he was looking at something. Lazarus glanced down and saw those bloody, battered fingers lying directly over the scar on his arm from the car accident. Only now, strangely, the burn looked like faint, torn finger marks.

The air split with a screech like tyres on wet tarmac, but it didn't come from the road. It came from inside the room. Red let go of Lazarus and turned sharply to the shadows in the corner. Lazarus heard bones creak as Red stretched his neck and said, 'My hounds are calling me. I must go.'

A thump of air barged through the lounge. It slammed

Lazarus up against the door. He slid to the floor like he'd been hit by a truck as he felt that same sick, dizzy ear-popping sensation he'd experienced in his bedroom and in the dining room.

The darkness in the corner of the room split like a bag filled with water, and Lazarus saw something more terrible than he could ever imagine on the other side.

5

☠ SLICK SLIME ☠

*H*ell . . . It was the only word that described it.

Lazarus stared at the thick blackness on the other side of the rip now hanging in midair in the corner of the room, fear like electricity burning through him. The rip looked like a hole in a curtain and its tattered edges flapped as though catching a faint breeze.

On the other side of the tear, a scene of such impossible violence nearly knocked Lazarus to the floor.

He could see . . . people. *The Dead*. Hundreds of them. They all had two arms, two legs, a head; but it was almost as if they were made of something not entirely solid. Their skin seemed to ripple, and it glistened, reminding Lazarus of fish he'd seen down the market. At points, they looked almost out of focus, like a picture on TV that wasn't quite tuned in right, fuzzy round the edges. But it was their eyes that really rapped his brain; they were a blinding white and shone with a torch-like intensity.

If these are the Dead, thought Lazarus, backing away from the rip, *then what the hell are those things tearing them apart?*

The creatures looked like something that lived in the sea, octopuses or squid with too many limbs, but they were at least the size of a small car. Their oily, wart-covered, mottled black skin shimmered in the firelight. And they had so many more tentacles, each one dripping in slime and split with thorn-like hooks. They were spinning and turning in and out of impossible knots, an ever-tumbling roll upon roll, slipping in and out of each other. And they were shredding the Dead, pulling them apart with a terrible and unstoppable frenzy. Each flick or twist of a tentacle sounded like a hosepipe snaking on the ground when no one's holding it, and as the Dead screamed, the things just kept on twisting and turning like knots of treacle-thick night.

Lazarus had a very bad feeling. Those things looked like they could, at any moment, just topple through the rip and then that would be his life over in a second. He quickly slipped over to the fireplace and grabbed the poker. It wasn't much, but it was better than nothing, and the heavy, blackened metal felt like some protection in his hand. His timing couldn't have been better. One of the tentacled things splashed into the room like a vast, silvery eel, flopped and thrashed about on the lounge floor like a dying fish, then headed straight for Red.

Red stood his ground like he was waiting for the thing to take him. Lazarus wanted to run but he just couldn't move; the fear had him and wouldn't let go.

He turned to Red, pointed through the rip. 'Are they . . . ?'

'Yes, Lazarus,' Red replied, and Lazarus saw just how grim his face had become. 'They are the Dead.'

The tentacled creature stopped in front of Red and sank to the ground, shivering.

'Then what the hell is that?' Lazarus shouted, pointing with the poker at the creature that was now reaching for Red with one of its tentacles.

Red reached out to the creature with his left hand. It was almost fully healed now, and looked only like a normal arm that had been put through a window, rather than one that had been peeled. The creature shivered as Red touched it.

'These, Lazarus,' said Red, 'are the creatures of oblivion. My pets, if you will. I am the guardian of all the realms of the Dead, and they?' Red grinned. 'They are my hounds!'

'Hounds?' said Lazarus. He knew what a dog looked like and it certainly wasn't like that.

Red nodded. 'I'm not supposed to be here, Lazarus. It was a tremendous risk for me to come through, but I had to see the Keeper, to at least get a message to him!'

Lazarus didn't know whether to scream or cry or yell. The rational side of his brain was fighting against the obvious in front of him.

Fallen angels don't exist! Hell doesn't exist! Those creatures, the Dead – none of this is real! It can't be! It just can't be!

'My pretties guarded the way for me,' said Red interrupting Lazarus's thoughts. 'None of the Dead could have passed them.' He laughed, and glanced at the unspeakable nightmare on the other side of the rip. 'Though as you can see, it doesn't stop them trying.'

Then something else fell through the rip and the rational side of Lazarus's brain gave up completely.

Oh God no . . .

There were three of them, three of the Dead. They were on the floor for a moment, a jumble of limbs, like young children trying to walk, but they were soon on their feet and Lazarus gasped.

The first was an old man, his back bent and his hair lost to nothing more than a few grey clumps. The second was a woman, slim, but with a neck stretched and twisted, her head lolling to one side. And the third looked only a few years older than Lazarus and was dressed in ruined motorbike leathers. They looked like they were covered in a slick slime. Lazarus knew they were after him, saw the hunger in their eyes.

The Dead glanced at Red, the creature at his feet, but swung straight back to Lazarus. He was all they were really interested in and when they grinned at him, their teeth were like obsidian shards.

Lazarus stumbled backwards and raised the poker, what little use it would do him. The Dead, however, just stood there, staring, their bodies swaying a little, like they were trying to stop themselves collapsing on the floor, their piercing white eyes burning into him with what

Lazarus could only describe as lust.

He looked at Red, looked back at the Dead. 'Don't touch me!' he screamed, jabbing the poker into the air. 'Don't bloody touch me!'

Lazarus knew he was about to be torn apart, ripped to pieces. He just knew it.

'Are you afraid, Lazarus?'

Lazarus turned to find Red staring at him, his face – now as much fresh skin as bloody wound – calm.

Lazarus said nothing, couldn't find his voice. Yes he was scared, but that word just didn't do justice to how he was feeling. Red was terrifying, the creature with him awful, but these things, *the Dead* ... The way they looked at Lazarus made him feel like his soul was being burned. And what terrified him the most was that they were so recognisable. They looked human, or as close as. Seeing Red and that thing with all the tentacles, he almost expected to be scared. But to see something so recognisably normal, and yet so unrecognisably horrifying, was beyond anything Lazarus could explain.

Lazarus wanted to run and run and run, yet he had a sense that, if he did, the Dead would follow and they would hunt him down and they would find him. And what they would do to him when they found him, he dared not think. But he had a fair idea.

Red jarred his thoughts. 'These are the Dead, Lazarus. Souls trapped by their wrongs, their lusts. Addicts.'

Lazarus remembered something from religious ed at school about a place between Heaven and Hell. It was – apparently – where souls were made ready for Heaven. But these things staring at him now . . . they didn't exactly look like Heaven was their final destination.

'You mean like purgatory?' he asked, impressed he could remember the correct name for it.

Red shook his head. 'The Dead aren't interested in redemption, Lazarus.'

Lazarus looked back at what Red had drawn on the mirror. 'So what about Hell?'

At this, Red's broken face shuddered. 'In Hell, Lazarus, even the Dead are afraid.'

The Dead moved forward a little, advancing together. They didn't stumble like the dead of Hollywood horror, thought Lazarus. These apparitions walked with purpose. And that purpose was him.

'Do you now understand why I had to come?' asked Red. 'Why I need you to tell your father all you have seen, all I have told you?'

'If you're asking if I'm scared, the answer's yes!' yelled Lazarus. 'I'll tell Dad everything, I promise!'

The Dead moved again, their faces yanked into horrible grins, their tongues black and dripping with grey spit. Lazarus felt like the main course in a restaurant he'd seen on TV where the diners got to choose what fish they wanted from a tank bubbling away against a wall.

Then they lunged at him.

Lazarus sprang backwards, sure as anything he was about to be pulled apart. Instead, he landed on the floor and saw the creature that had been with Red slip across the room and wrap itself round the Dead.

Screams and howls filled the air as they were pulled limb from limb and tossed back through the rip. Some bits didn't quite make it and thumped against the lounge walls with the sound of jelly. Others landed in the fire to spit and burn, filling the room with the sweet smell of barbecued pork. Lazarus felt fluids splashing over him, warm against his skin. But even more disturbing was the sound Red was making. It was a hollow laugh and it bounced around the room, refusing to quieten.

He's enjoying this, Lazarus realised.

Red's voice echoed in the room. 'You cannot kill that which is already dead, Lazarus,' he said, as what was left of the Dead stilled on the floor. 'Death is nothing more than a change of scenery.'

'But what that thing just did,' said Lazarus. 'It ripped them apart!'

'And in time,' said Red, 'they will again find the strength to create a form to occupy. It takes them centuries, but that doesn't stop them trying. Where they exist, in a sunless and eternal place, time is irrelevant.'

Lazarus pushed himself to his feet, felt for the door handle, pulled it hard, but it wouldn't budge. He tried again; nothing. He thought about what Red had said as he gave it another yank. It sounded like Red was telling him that no matter what anyone did, the Dead would always return. Then how could you ever stop them?

'But why do they bother?' he asked. 'What's in it for them?'

The look Red let slip across his face made Lazarus

stumble backwards against the wall.

'You are,' he said through a chilling smile. 'The Dead envy the living. It consumes them. They will do anything to take what you have, for even the briefest of moments, to experience life again.'

Lazarus saw Red stretch his left arm out to point at the door, then open his hand. The lounge door flew open and Lazarus felt himself ripped out of the room. He landed hard on the tiles of the hallway floor, cracking his head, his right shoulder, his breath slamming from him.

Red's voice was a tornado and it tore through the house. 'Remember!' he called, staring at Lazarus through the open door. 'Tell your father! The Dead are coming and Hell is coming with them!'

Then the lounge door banged shut so hard that cracks snaked instantly across the wall, and plaster fell to the floor.

Screams and crashes and howls tore the air. The lounge door was shaking, like it was on the verge of splintering into wooden shards. The sound clawed at Lazarus, piercing his skin like fish hooks, forcing him to crawl away from it across the floor, his hands over his ears, his eyes shut, his forehead scraping along the tiles, desperate for the sound to end.

Then silence, the sound sucked away to nothing in an instant. And once again, like he was on an aeroplane plunging through an air pocket, Lazarus felt his ears pop, his head spin, and his stomach churn.

6

HORRIFIC NIGHTMARE

Lazarus woke up yelling one word over and over again.

'DAD! DAD! DAD!'

When he stopped, the only sound was that of his heart banging hard against his ribs. It was the kind of heartbeat he only ever achieved running from trouble. And he'd done that a lot. But he'd run from nothing like the images now piling into his mind from the night before.

Lazarus closed his eyes, let his head fall forward, rubbed his forehead. What the hell had happened last night? What kind of nightmare was that? He felt utterly, completely exhausted. And he was covered in sweat; he could feel the heat rising from his skin, the sheets on his bed sticking to him. Sitting up, his whole body ached, but deep breaths calmed him down. Images from the nightmare flickered in his mind, like a badly recorded movie he wasn't supposed to watch.

Lazarus remembered being in the kitchen, chatting to Craig, having a snack. But when on earth had he come to bed? His mind was blank except for flashbacks to the impossible, horrific nightmare, which ended with him being thrown out of the lounge and landing on the floor.

The sound of a car driving past, some birds nattering about the night they'd had, calmed Lazarus even more; everything was normal here. No odd smell. No rips between worlds. No insane visions of nightmares come to life. No hint of the Dead or creatures of oblivion or Red asking after his dad.

Dad ...

Lazarus shook his head, sucked in cool air, realised it was morning. Whatever he'd dreamt last night, his best guess was that it was simply brought about by too much caffeine, cheese on toast and dodgy horror movies: enough to give anyone vivid nightmares. He wondered what Craig would have to say about it. He'd probably take notes and turn it into a story. Then take the piss.

Bright sun streamed through his window, across his

desk and on to the floor, forming a puddle of warm light. Lazarus reached out to his desk for his phone to call Craig. It wasn't there.

He scratched his head, yawned, and sat up, swinging his feet out of bed and on to the floor. They splashed in the warm sunlight pouring through his window. He looked over to his desk. His alarm clock read 07:30.

Over at the speaker unit for his MP3, Lazarus found himself remembering the nightmares he used to have as a young boy. He couldn't remember any images, not any more, but the feelings they pulled from him he could still recall: a sense that all hope was gone and that he was utterly alone, a deep red darkness everywhere . . . Dad had always told him the nightmares were because of the crash, nothing more, that they'd go away in time. And they had.

The memory sent a shiver through his body. Goosebumps pimpled his skin. Rubbing his eyes, Lazarus reached over to the speaker unit, turned it up and pressed PLAY. Music stung the morning as he headed to the bathroom. The crazy dreams or whatever they were had made him feel groggy and he knew a sure-fire way to sort that out was a damned good shower and some suitably zingy shower gel. Followed swiftly by a fried egg butty with cheese and chilli sauce.

Guitars and drums rammed through the air. At the bathroom sink Lazarus splashed cold water on to his face and looked at his reflection. OK, so he'd looked better. But then again, he'd looked a whole lot worse.

Lazarus reached out to get the shower started, then looked back at the open bathroom door as a thought struck him. It was a small thing, but Lazarus needed to know where his phone was. He always put it on his desk before going to sleep. It was a little ritual. And in the dream, hadn't he dropped it in the lounge? Perhaps it was still there.

Lazarus walked out of the bathroom and down the stairs. He told himself he was just going to make sure he hadn't lost his phone and that it was exactly where he thought it was. He certainly wasn't heading down to the lounge to see if it was still in one piece. That would be nuts.

The morning light basted the house with an almost olive gold from the window over the stairs. There wasn't a smell to make him chuck up. And everything was quiet but for the ticking of clocks, which echoed hypnotically in the air.

Craig is going to love this, thought Lazarus, as the ground-floor hallway drew close. It was the kind of stuff he absolutely lived for: weird dreams, ghosts and ghouls.

Something caused Lazarus to stop a couple of steps from the bottom of the stairs. A change in sound. What was it? The clocks. Something was different. Then he realised – one of them had stopped. That was something his dad never allowed to happen. The clocks only ever stopped if he was cleaning them, making sure they were fine. And he always checked to make sure they were fully wound before he went away. He must've forgotten one. Now that was a first.

Lazarus stepped on to the cold tiles in the hallway and turned to the lounge door with a yawn. It was only when the door was fully open, when he spotted his phone on the rug, that he saw the bookcase, or what was left of it.

It was in pieces across the floor.

A flashback of Red's wing slamming through it burst like a firework inside his head. He turned and saw a scorched line through brickwork on the other side of the room where Red's other wing had raked across it. Bloody footprints were on the carpet. On the rocking chair by the fire a thick red stain dripped from the seat, down the legs and on to the floor. The fire was still smouldering, a faint grey wisp slipping silently up the chimney.

Like watching a movie on fast-forward, the reality of the nightmare crashed through Lazarus's mind. He remembered every last bit of it and had to brace himself against an armchair to stop himself stumbling forward.

At last, the images stopped. Lazarus breathed, gulped air fast.

But it couldn't have been real, he thought. *It was impossible and wrong and ...*

... and then, as he turned to leave the room, he saw the mirror above the fire. Two bloody circles stared back at him, exactly how he remembered Red drawing them, only hours before, when he'd been telling him to contact his father.

The metallic smell of the blood hit the back of Lazarus's throat. He gagged, doubled over, grabbed the armchair again to stop himself collapsing, and threw up. Panting, hair stuck to his sweaty forehead, he leant on his arms. He hadn't made it up. He hadn't dreamt it.

It was all for real.

Lazarus slowly straightened up, waited for his head to stop swimming, then picked up his phone. He flicked through the menu and found some messages. He couldn't be bothered to check them; they were all from one number, Craig. But he had to phone someone else, someone he never phoned. Ever.

Dad . . .

Lazarus tapped speed dial.

Waited.

But all he got was the answer phone.

He tried again. Only this time he heard something elsewhere in the house – another phone was ringing.

Lazarus dashed out of the lounge and into the hall, shutting his own phone on the way. The sound of the other phone died.

For a few seconds, Lazarus stood in the hallway, listening for anything, trying to work out where the sound of the phone had come from. He hadn't liked the way the ringing had vanished as soon as he'd hung up himself.

Lazarus raised his own phone again and punched in his dad's number.

He heard the other phone buzz back in answer. Keeping

his own phone open, Lazarus followed the sound and found himself at the door of his dad's study. He went to knock, simply out of habit, then twisted the handle and pushed the door open. The ringing grew louder. Lazarus walked to his dad's desk. He pulled the centre drawer open. And there, vibrating and ringing inside, was his father's phone.

Lazarus reached in, flipped it open, saw his own name on the screen. *Dad hasn't taken his phone with him*, he thought. And in that moment he felt awfully, terribly alone.

Frustration and anger grabbed him. Lazarus snapped the phone shut and threw it across the room. It clattered against the wall, dropped to the floor. He put his hands to his head, pulled at his hair. He felt like he was going insane.

His own phone trilled into the moment.

'Dad? Dad! Is that you?'

Of course it wasn't, he thought. *How could it be?*

It was Craig.

'What the hell happened to you?'

Lazarus wasn't about to explain. 'Get over here now,' he said. 'You're not going to believe this.'

7
BLOODY FOOTPRINTS

'**W**ell?'

For the past five minutes, Craig had stared at the damage to the lounge, mouth open, voice stilled.

At last he looked back at Lazarus. 'You found the lounge like that this morning?'

Lazarus nodded.

'And you're sure someone didn't break in and do the place over while you were asleep?'

'I think I'd have heard, don't you?'

Craig nodded and said, 'Now I'm only asking this because we need to be sure, but . . .' He paused.

'What?' said Lazarus.

'Did you do it?'

Lazarus stared at him. 'Are you serious?'

'Just making sure,' said Craig, holding his hands up in

defence. 'People do the weirdest stuff. And I'm your mate and what's in *there* doesn't make any sense at all. You could've done it and blanked it from your mind or something. What you said you saw, it's all pretty nuts, isn't it?'

'I didn't make it up,' protested Lazarus. 'It was real.'

When Craig had arrived, Lazarus hadn't given him a chance to speak. Instead, he'd just opened the front door and said, 'Shut up and follow me.' He'd warned Craig about what was in the lounge, laid it on real thick, but Craig, despite his best efforts, hadn't really believed a word of it. That was until he'd walked into the room and seen it for himself.

Craig had pushed his glasses up over his forehead and stared at the room, mouth open, speechless. For a few moments he'd seemed frozen to the spot, then eventually he'd walked slowly in.

Lazarus watched Craig as he again looked from the bloody footprints on the floor to the smashed bookcase then back at him, his right hand involuntarily scratching his head. His fingers got tangled in the mop of red hair that seemed to burst from his head like it was desperate to escape.

Craig eventually said, 'So what are you going to do?'

'What can I do?' shrugged Lazarus. 'I guess I'd better call the police or something. All that blood . . .'

'The police?' said Craig, his voice almost rising an octave. 'Are you mental?'

'Look around you!' snapped Lazarus. 'There's blood everywhere! The police need to know!'

'And when you tell them what happened, what then?' demanded Craig. 'How are you going to explain those creatures you think you saw? How are you going to describe this Red bloke?'

'What choice do I have?' Lazarus knew he was shouting, but he didn't care. At that moment it was the only thing that made him feel better.

'They'll see this and think you've dragged someone back here and chain-sawed them to pieces,' said Craig. 'They'll lock you up first and ask questions later!'

Lazarus was grasping at anything to explain what had happened, something reasonable, something tangible. 'Perhaps I did make some of it up. Perhaps that was the only way for my brain to deal with what happened.'

'Seems a bit far-fetched, don't you think?' said Craig.

'The whole thing is far-fetched!' Lazarus snapped. 'A bloke with no skin? Killer octopuses falling out of the air? It's insane!'

'Strictly speaking, it's octopodes,' said Craig. 'Not octopuses.'

'Shut up!' snarled Lazarus.

'OK,' shrugged Craig, 'but you can't call the police. Seriously, mate. That would be well stupid. And what about all that stuff this Red bloke spoke about?'

'What – the whole *the Dead are coming* thing? Hell?'

'Exactly that,' said Craig. 'You'll just sound like a horror-freak teenager who's been smoking a few dodge fags.'

'So what about Dad leaving his mobile here?'

'What about it?' Craig replied.

'Well where is he?' Lazarus demanded. 'Why did he leave it? Where's he gone? What about all that stuff about Dad being a Keeper?'

'I don't mean to be out of order,' said Craig, 'but we're talking about your dad here, right? The bloke who advises on security in the day and plays with old timepieces at night? The bloke who never speaks to you? The bloke whose idea of a good night out is to stay in and mend the chime on a cuckoo clock?'

Lazarus opened his mouth to say something, but nothing came to mind, so he shut it again. Speaking to Craig about it all had simply confirmed one thing: he was going insane.

Lazarus looked at his mate. 'So what do you suggest?'

'You're not going to like it,' warned Craig.

'I don't like you,' said Lazarus, 'but we've hung out together for far too long now to do anything about it.'

Craig strolled over to look at the bloody rings drawn on the mirror and Lazarus wondered if Craig had ever been uptight about anything. No matter what happened in his life, he seemed to take it all with the same ah-whatever attitude. If the world was about to end, Craig would have a positive spin on it and nip out for doughnuts before the final conflagration.

'I know some people,' said Craig. 'They might be able to help.'

Lazarus knew straight away where this was going and he didn't want to be any part of it.

'No way. You're not on about that local ghost freaks group you've joined, are you?'

'It's paranormal investigators,' said Craig, with the emphasis on *paranormal*. 'And they're not freaks.'

'They let you join.'

'Ha ha,' said Craig.

Lazarus shook his head. 'You can't be serious. I don't believe in any of that stuff. You know that. It's all just over-active imaginations and people's brains playing tricks on them. Dead's dead, mate. Anything else is just wishful thinking and weirdos on *Most Haunted* scaring each other in the dark.'

'That doesn't explain your lounge,' pointed out Craig. 'You really think any of this is because you've got an over-active imagination?'

Lazarus said nothing. He didn't want anyone else finding out about this. Certainly not those idiots Craig took seriously.

'And they're not weirdos,' said Craig. 'They're just normal people who think there's more to paranormal stuff than ghost stories round a camp fire.'

'Nutters,' said Lazarus.

'You're the one with the visions of the Dead and a lounge covered in blood,' said Craig.

Lazarus knew Craig had a point, but he still wasn't happy. Telling his best mate all about the night before was hard enough. But having a bunch of strangers walk in and start doing ouija boards and stuff? That was too much for anyone to deal with.

'But what if I did do all this myself?' said Lazarus, even if he didn't actually believe it. 'What if I had a shocker of a nightmare, did this, and then knocked myself out? Maybe I just don't remember it?'

'I'm guessing,' said Craig, 'that you'd remember where the blood came from.'

Lazarus didn't reply and instead walked over to the lounge window. The world looked normal out there. But that just made the state of the lounge seem even more stark.

'Look,' said Craig, giving a shrug, 'why not just see what happens? If it comes to nothing, go to the police. But give it a go. What have you got to lose?'

Lazarus turned back from the window. 'You're loving this aren't you?' he said bitterly.

Craig smiled and shrugged. 'They're OK people. Some are a bit weird – that comes with the territory –

but a few are pretty normal.'

'For *Ghostbusters*,' muttered Lazarus. 'So who you gonna call?'

Craig laughed at the movie reference. He left the room and was back from the hallway in a second, his battered leather satchel in his arms.

'That really is the worst bag ever,' said Lazarus, attempting to cling on to some sense of normality. If it was just the two of them messing around then he could almost tell himself that nothing had changed, life was just as it always was. Dull. Boring. A case of living through school until it was time to leave. He remembered Craig's invite for a few days kicking around at his parents' caravan. That conversation seemed like days ago, weeks almost. 'You look like an idiot with it, like you're just starting school or something.'

'It's my writer's bag,' said Craig, opening it dramatically and ignoring the mocking tone in Lazarus's voice. 'Helps me focus on the fact that writing is what I want to do with my life. Contains everything I need: pens, notebooks, net book, *Writers' and Artists' Yearbook* . . . And check this out!'

Lazarus took the book that Craig slipped out from his bag. He wasn't exactly impressed. '*Haunted Somerset?* Oooh, creepy . . .'

Craig nodded. 'Loads of stuff in there,' he said, pulling out his phone and keying up the contacts list. 'Really interesting.'

'You don't have them on speed dial, do you?' asked Lazarus in disbelief.

Craig nodded and smiled, then started a conversation with whoever answered.

While Craig was talking Lazarus flicked through the book and wasn't convinced it was interesting at all. It seemed to be nothing more than a few rubbish black and white photographs and some 'apparently true' stories by 'first-hand witnesses'.

He looked back at Craig, who was still on the phone, and handed the book back. It was going to take more than that to convince him a world existed beyond the grave.

Craig hung up.

'So?' said Lazarus. 'Who've you just told about all this?'

'I've not told anyone anything,' said Craig. 'That was Clair Vine.'

'Her real name or one she uses to make sure she sounds really weird?'

Craig shook his head and said, 'You'll like her, I promise. She's one of the younger members of the group and seems pretty switched on.'

'But what did you tell her? I don't want everyone in town knowing about this!'

'I know that, you idiot,' said Craig. 'I've just said that I'd a mate who wanted to know more about the group and if she'd be happy to come round for a chat.'

'Forgive me if I don't get all excited,' said Lazarus.

Craig didn't reply.

8
☠ SHATTERED GLASS ☠

Half an hour later the doorbell rang. Lazarus and Craig had left the lounge and gone through to the kitchen for a drink and a bite. Lazarus wasn't even hungry, he thought, as they leant against the cupboards, chatting about nothing. But it did a little to take his mind off whatever it was that was going on. Trouble was, getting Red – who or whatever he was, his voice, his smell, his face – out of his head was next to impossible.

'That'll be her,' said Craig.

'Do I need to get any candles and incense?' joked Lazarus. 'Spooks love all that hippy shit, don't they?'

'Just go get the door,' said Craig throwing a packet of biscuits at Lazarus's head.

Lazarus caught the biscuits. 'You phoned her,' he said, 'so you can go get her. This is all your idea.'

He wasn't sure, now that someone had actually turned up, that he wanted to go through with this at all.

'But she's come to see you,' said Craig.

'Then you'd better hurry up then, hadn't you?'

Craig put down his almost empty mug. 'Remember she didn't have to come. And I know you don't believe any of all this, but just give it a chance, right? It's not like we've been able to come up with a rational explanation, is it?'

Lazarus nodded. 'I'll see you in the lounge.'

They walked out of the kitchen and down the hall. At the lounge door Craig turned right, heading for the front door. Lazarus went to push open the door to the lounge, but hesitated. The cracks around the doorframe made the walls look like shattered glass. *They happened when I was thrown out of the room*, he thought, remembering the sound the door made when it slammed shut, like it was about to fly off its hinges. Something deep down was telling him that what was on the other side was more than just a nightmare, but the rational side of him was trying to ignore it. Lazarus knew if he walked in there, the something-deep-down would win out.

He turned away from the lounge and joined Craig at

the front door, just as he was opening it. He blinked. The person now standing in front of him wasn't exactly like the image he'd created in his mind.

'This is Clair Vine,' said Craig. 'Clair, this is—'

'Lazarus,' said Clair and she reached out her hand. 'Hi!'

'Hi,' said Lazarus, and couldn't really think of anything else to add. He'd expected a freak show to turn up at the door. Someone all decked out in bangles and patchwork clothing – all that stupid stuff he hated. Instead, Clair was normal. There was nothing exceptional about her at all. She looked early twenties, had shoulder-length brown hair and sparkly grey eyes, was wearing jeans, trainers and a hooded top and had a small rucksack slung over her shoulder. She didn't look, thought Lazarus, anything like the kind of person – particularly being a girl – who'd be spending her time as a ghostbuster.

'Cool house,' said Clair, looking around her as Craig allowed her to come in. 'I'm well jealous.'

'Try living here,' said Lazarus. 'It's not cool. It's freezing.'

'Adds to the romance, though,' Clair replied. 'Who

wants a new house? Got no soul those places; this has history. You can feel it.'

'I guess,' said Lazarus. To him the place was just a house. And, if he was honest, he couldn't wait until he was old enough to leave.

Lazarus then looked over at Craig as Clair moved past him into the house, and whispered, 'Do you actually know her?'

'Ha ha,' said Craig, without smiling. 'Of course I do.'

'But she's . . . normal.'

'What were you expecting?' asked Craig. 'A crystal ball and a black cape?'

Lazarus shrugged. 'That's not what I meant.'

He turned to shut the door, but he saw something that made him stop. At the end of the front garden, on the other side of the street, someone in a long and scruffy ankle-length coat, either brown or just really badly stained, was staring at his house.

Lazarus stood for a moment in the shadow of the front door. The person was tall, but Lazarus couldn't make out if it was a man or a woman. He could see dark, lank shoulder-length hair, but that was about it.

Lazarus frowned. Why were they just staring like that? What did they want? He was half tempted to go and find out, but Craig's voice called from the lounge and he went through.

Craig and Clair were sitting on the three-seater sofa. The room was exactly as Lazarus had left it, though thanks to him opening the windows when he'd taken Craig in there earlier that morning, the air wasn't as rich with the sweet smell of blood. If anything, the smell had pretty much gone, which struck him as odd.

Lazarus sat down on a footstool and looked at Clair and Craig.

Clair gestured at the room with a look and said, 'And you found it like this?'

Lazarus nodded.

'Did anyone else hear what happened?'

Lazarus shook his head. 'Dad's away on business,' he said. 'God knows how I'm going to explain all this if I can't repair that bookshelf or get the blood out.'

'Tell me what happened,' said Clair, and Lazarus could see that although her eyes were wide and bright and open, her face was deadly serious. 'And I need you to be as clear and detailed as you can, OK? Don't leave anything out.'

'Some of it's a bit nuts,' said Lazarus, hesitating. 'I mean, I hardly believe any of it myself.'

'Doesn't matter,' insisted Clair. 'Just tell me.'

When Lazarus had finished, he felt strangely tired, like going back over everything that had happened had exhausted him. He looked over at Craig, who'd busied himself taking notes the whole time Lazarus was talking, and then at Clair. Her eyes hadn't left him once and their blinking had become almost hypnotic. At first it had felt a bit odd, to speak to this woman he'd never met before about something he couldn't explain, but as he'd continued talking it had felt as though those eyes were dragging the words from him.

'Well?' he asked finally, standing up from the stool to stretch his legs. 'What do you think? What is it? A poltergeist? A ghost? What? Or am I just mental? Am I about to lose my mind and go out on a murder spree?' He tried to sound flippant, to act like he didn't really care. Because if he did care, it made things just a little too real.

For a moment, Clair just sat there, holding her Coke

can between her hands. *Either she's trying to think up an excuse to run the hell away*, thought Lazarus, *or she's just being polite and doesn't know how to tell me that I'm a mentalist.*

At last, Clair looked up.

'Well?'

'To be honest, Lazarus, I've never heard anything like it.'

'Thanks,' Lazarus sighed. 'That makes me feel so much better.'

'No, seriously,' said Clair, sitting forward. 'It's the most amazing thing I've ever heard! What do you think, Craig?'

'Totally,' said Craig. 'There's no way he could make it up. I've known him for years; his imagination just isn't that clever.'

'That's what I like most about you,' said Lazarus. 'The unwavering support. But now what?'

Clair stood up and walked to the corner of the room where Lazarus had seen the rip. 'This is where you saw that portal, right?'

'I never called it a portal,' said Lazarus, desperate to

distance himself from anything that sounded like he was taking this seriously. 'And at no point did I use any kind of language to suggest that any of this is for real. It was a rip or a tear, like in a curtain or something.'

'But this was where it was, right? Where you saw those creatures and the Dead?'

Lazarus nodded. 'I don't know what they were,' he said. 'I just told you what I saw, and that's it. Perhaps Craig is right. Perhaps I've watched too many of his crappy horror movies.'

'This is better than the movies,' said Clair, and Lazarus could see the excitement in her face. 'I mean, this is a real chance to make contact with the other side!'

'You what?'

Lazarus couldn't believe what he was hearing – it sounded like Clair wasn't just interested in finding out what had happened, but communicating with what he'd seen. He'd no idea how she was going to do it and he was absolutely sure he didn't want to find out.

'Don't you see, Lazarus?' said Clair, her hands raised to where Lazarus had seen the rip. 'This could be the most amazing paranormal event in history! Here! In your house!'

'No, I don't see,' said Lazarus. 'All I want is to know what might have happened, that's all. I don't want anything to do with experiencing any of that again. Ever. Got it?'

The only answer he got was a smile from Clair and a shrug from Craig.

He knew they weren't listening.

9

INTRUDER

'I don't want anything to do with this.'

Lazarus had watched as Clair had pulled from her bag about a dozen small candles in little clay jars and laid them in a circle on the carpet under where he'd seen the rip, then lit them. Craig had been all too happy to help and the two of them were now sitting inside the circle and talking excitedly.

'Whatever it is you're doing, I'm not taking part,' said Lazarus.

'What's up?' asked Craig. 'You scared?'

Lazarus snapped up at this. He wasn't scared of anything. Except perhaps what he'd experienced the night before, real or not.

'I've done this before,' said Clair, getting herself comfortable on the floor, her legs crossed. 'All I'm going to do is knock on a door. I'm not going to open it.'

'I don't actually give a damn,' said Lazarus. 'You go ahead and make yourselves look like complete tits. I'm going to sit this one out.'

'You sure?'

Lazarus nodded and Clair turned back to Craig.

'Right,' she said, 'I'm just going to attempt to contact the other side.'

'Oooh, how creepy,' said Lazarus, eyes raised.

Trouble was, deep down he knew that the reason he was taking the piss was because he was more than a little scared of what Clair and Craig were now doing. It felt very, very wrong. It wasn't that he believed it would work, that Clair would manage to do anything except make Craig feel happy, but that he couldn't get away from the niggling feeling that if it did, something bad would happen. And after the night before, the word 'bad' had taken on a whole new meaning.

Clair's voice interrupted Lazarus's thoughts, but he couldn't make out what she was saying; it sounded prayer-like, but her voice was little more than a mumble.

'What's she saying?' Lazarus asked, looking over at Craig.

Craig shrugged. 'Sounds cool though, doesn't it?'

'I don't think this is a good idea,' said Lazarus. 'It's just stupid. We'd be better off just cleaning up and forgetting about it all.'

'Shush!' hissed Craig. 'You'll spoil it!'

'Spoil what?' sniffed Lazarus. 'This is total bollocks, you know that, don't you? Everything I saw was a nightmare. That's the only explanation. I had a nightmare and went sleep-walking. That's why I don't remember causing any of this damage. I've no idea yet about the blood, but I'm sure there's a rational explanation for it, too. But that's all any of this was.'

Craig went to reply but a crash sounded through the house. He was on his feet in an instant.

'What the hell was that?'

'Came from the front of the house,' said Lazarus, alert.

'You mean your dad's study?' said Craig.

'Probably a cat outside or something,' said Clair, remaining on the floor in the circle of candles and sounding a little irritated. 'I'm going to have to start all over again now.'

'That's no cat,' said Lazarus. 'For a start, we don't

own one, unless Dad bought a lion and didn't tell me about it. And anyway, that came from inside the house, not outside.'

Clair had started chanting again.

'She seems normal,' Lazarus nodded to Craig, 'but she's a fruit.'

'Takes all sorts,' said Craig. 'You think that sound's some idiot trying to break in?'

'Reckon so. And that's the last thing I need with all this crap to deal with as well.'

Lazarus was angry now. Trying to deal with what had happened in the lounge was one thing, but if some prat was breaking in, he wouldn't be held responsible for his actions if he got a hold of them. Pact or no pact with his dad.

'Just a thought,' said Craig, hesitating. 'If it is someone breaking in, do you really think it's a good idea to go out there and tackle them?'

Lazarus picked something up from the floor. It was the poker from the fireplace. He pushed to the back of his mind the memory of the last time he'd held it and why and said, 'I'm going to make them regret waking up with the idea of even coming here in the first place.'

Lazarus yanked open the door and ran into the hallway, the poker already raised for an attack. After everything that had happened, the confusion, the fear, the panic, he was just in the mood for a good scrap. Craig was fast on his heels, a piece of the broken bookshelf in his own hands.

Lazarus had no plan of attack. Instead, he just crashed through his dad's study door, Craig right behind him. As the door flew open, they both stood there, primitive weapons raised.

For a moment, the room looked empty. Then Lazarus saw the open window and movement behind his dad's desk. The drawers of the desk were open, letters and papers and whatever else they'd contained scattered all over the floor. And someone was standing over a smashed desk lamp.

Lazarus recognised the stranger he'd seen staring at the house when Clair had turned up. He'd known something wasn't right then and now here they were. They must've been scoping the place out for a bit of breaking and entering.

Lazarus gripped the poker so hard his knuckles turned white. He saw Craig do the same with the piece of wood and was immediately impressed with his friend. They'd never been in a fight together before, but it was pretty reassuring to know Craig was someone he could depend on, no questions asked.

No one moved. No one spoke.

Lazarus ground the silence between his teeth.

'I saw you watching the house earlier,' he said, his voice filled with menace. 'Who the hell are you?'

The person didn't speak. Lazarus still wasn't sure if it was a man or a woman. He or she was tall, thin and the grubby-looking coat and long dark hair disguised any possible means of identification.

'Whatever it is you're looking for, you can't have it,' Lazarus went on. 'You hear me?'

The intruder had something in one hand. It was a book.

'Put that down,' Lazarus roared. 'Put it down and back off, right? I mean it.'

The person in the coat didn't move. To Lazarus it didn't seem as though he or she was in any way scared. It felt almost as though this person would have no problem dealing with whatever he and Craig could do, and walk away utterly unscathed.

'I said put the book down and back off,' repeated Lazarus.

The person slipped the book into a coat pocket.

'You shouldn't have done that,' said Lazarus, his blood close to boiling. 'You really shouldn't have.'

But as he moved forward, the person spun with such speed towards the open window that neither Lazarus nor Craig had time to react. And then they were gone, having dived head-first through the gap.

Lazarus dashed to the window, then turned out of the room, flew to the front door and ran out into the front garden. But the stranger was gone.

Craig came out after him. 'That was totally impossible!' he exclaimed. 'To just jump through the window like that. Unbelievable.'

Lazarus didn't have an answer. It was just another weird thing to add to an already super weird twenty-four hours.

'Come on,' he said grimly, 'let's go see if anything else other than that book is missing.'

It didn't take Lazarus long to realise that, thankfully, the only thing missing was the book – and that it was nothing more than his dad's most recent diary.

'But why nick that?' said Lazarus, slumping down in his dad's office chair. 'What's the point?'

Craig shrugged. 'Maybe he just grabbed the first thing to hand when we disturbed him. You know, didn't want to leave empty-handed.'

'I guess.' Lazarus considered it. 'Still doesn't make sense though, does it?' He motioned at the desk with his hand. 'It even looks like he was actually here to find that diary – nothing of value's been taken, and the only stuff that's been disturbed is Dad's papers and stuff.'

'You reckon he knows your dad?'

'How should I know? But if he was after the diary, then he must've been trying to find out something about Dad. But what? What would a diary tell him?'

'Where your dad is,' suggested Craig.

Lazarus looked at Craig. 'And why would anyone other than me need to know where Dad is?'

Craig said nothing.

'Best of luck to whoever that was,' said Lazarus. 'Perhaps

they'll have better luck contacting him than me.'

He thought back to finding his dad's mobile in the desk a few hours ago. That sense of being so very alone swept over him again.

'Come on,' he said, pulling himself out of his dad's chair. 'Lets finish off with Clair and then decide what to do about this, OK? It's not like we can call the police over a stolen diary, is it?'

Craig nodded. 'Not really, no.'

They left the study and walked back to the lounge, Lazarus first. But when they entered, Clair wasn't sitting in the circle of candles; she was standing up, her hand tracing an impossible, inky black circular line in the air that was seeping darkness into the lounge.

A line Lazarus knew was the exact place he'd seen the rip appear the night before.

10

💀💀💀 DEATHLY PALE 💀💀💀

Lazarus didn't wait for Craig. He dashed across the room to Clair.

'What the hell are you doing?' he screamed, his eyes on the black line in the air. It seemed to float there like a thin trail of smoke, except that in places the two sides of the line were starting to peel apart like a zipper.

Clair didn't respond. Her finger just kept on tracing in the air. Lazarus could see that soon the two ends of the line would meet. And he really didn't want to even guess at what could happen if they did. He'd seen this before, but Red had been here then, protected him from the Dead. But this time, they were alone.

He turned back to Craig.

'Do you know what she's done? Or how she's doing this? Why can't she hear me? What do we do?'

Craig's face was blank. 'I don't know,' he shrugged. 'I mean, I've seen Clair do stuff like this before, you know all the candles and chanting, but nothing like that!'

'And that's supposed to make me feel better? I thought you knew all about this stuff?'

'Clair knows what she's doing,' said Craig, his voice shaking a little. 'At least I'm sure she does. She's not in to this because it's freaky or scary. She's just interested in the afterlife and ghosts.'

'That doesn't explain what she's doing now, does it?' snapped Lazarus, pointing at Clair.

Craig looked at him, shook his head and said, 'No, I guess not.'

Lazarus knew he had to do something. Looking back at Clair, at the line in the air, he could picture the rip, or portal, or whatever it was that had appeared in the room the night before.

'You need to stop!' he pleaded. 'You don't know what you're doing, what you're playing with! I've seen what's on the other side of this. Trust me, you really don't want to see it too.'

Clair did nothing but smile and continue with the line.

Lazarus knew she hadn't a clue what she was doing; her eyes were somewhere else, like she was staring through a haze of drugs. He was beginning to panic now. The edges of the line were peeling further and further apart, Clair's finger working like a knife cutting a hole in a large sheet of paper. And the piece of air inside the line was beginning to flap; Lazarus could feel a dry heat wafting over him.

Lazarus grabbed hold of Clair's top and pulled. She didn't move. Not an inch. It was like she was stone. He pulled again, then tried pushing, but it was no good. Whatever it was that Clair had started, she couldn't control. Someone – some*thing* – else was running this show now. Lazarus didn't dare imagine what.

On the floor were the remains of the shelves from the bookcase. Lazarus ran over, picked one up, then turned back to Clair. When he raised the plank of wood, he paused for a second. Was he really going to smack her one? Was that really the only way to stop what she'd started?

The questions died as a familiar stench leaked into the room. Lazarus felt his head swim, had to stop himself falling to the floor. Bile was in his throat and he had to focus hard to not throw up. Something was coming . . . he just knew it. Something from the other side of what Clair had just opened.

Then Lazarus saw something push through the nearly complete hole in the air. And he knew he'd seen something like it before.

It was one of the Dead.

A thin arm with tallowy skin flopped over the edge of the hole and grabbed on to Clair. She howled in pain. Lazarus saw its fingers dig into her skin. The rest of the Dead's body was following. A head was coming through now. It reminded him of the photos they'd all seen at school during sex education: pictures of a woman giving birth.

It's now or never, thought Lazarus. *Even if this doesn't work, there's nothing else I can do.*

He raised the plank.

'NO!'

Lazarus turned to see Craig running towards him.

'You can't hit her with that!' he yelled. 'You can't! It'll kill her!'

But Lazarus had made up his mind. With every ounce

of his strength, he brought the plank of wood down. It slammed into the arm slipping out through the hole. The force Lazarus had used sent him off balance and he toppled forward. A squeal from the other side of the hole shot out into the room. Craig dropped to the floor, his hands holding his ears. Clair screamed. Lazarus saw that the hand was still holding on; it didn't want to let go of Clair, not one bit. Without a second thought, he brought the plank up high, then smashed it down again. The arm crunched under the impact. Lazarus saw it buckle. The squeal grew louder, then another sound joined it: a flapping, wet sound. A tentacle flashed out from the other side of the hole, wrapped itself round the arm, and pulled.

The arm tore off. A splash of black and red burst in the portal like a balloon filled with paint. Then the portal collapsed on itself.

Clair dropped like liquid. Lazarus caught her before she totalled it on the floor, but only just. They both landed on top of the candles, snuffing them out and kicking hot wax everywhere.

For a while the only thing Lazarus could hear was the sound of his own breathing as his nausea faded. Then

Clair's voice slipped into the air.

'What . . . happened?'

Lazarus pushed himself up on to his knees. He was angry. Clair had messed with stuff she hadn't a clue about, that was more than obvious. But at least she'd clarified the fact that he was actually sane and hadn't made any of the previous night up.

Lazarus wasn't sure if that was a good thing or not.

'You had no idea what you were doing, did you?' he screamed.

'It's not that,' said Clair faintly and Lazarus could see sweat beading all over her face, like she'd just jumped off a treadmill. 'Something else happened. I don't know what it was.'

'I'm not interested,' Lazarus snapped back. 'But at least I know I'm not nuts!'

'What the hell was that?'

It was Craig, his face pale and sweating.

'That was a little taster of last night's main event,' Lazarus said, seeing the fear in his friend's eyes. 'Clair here opened up a hole to wherever it was that Red and everything else I saw came from.'

'But that's impossible!' Craig exclaimed then turned on Clair. 'What did you do? I thought you knew what you were doing!'

'Apparently not,' Lazarus replied. He looked back at Clair. 'You OK?'

Clair pulled herself up from the floor and dusted herself down, but the movement caused her to lose balance and she quickly reached for the wall. 'I think so,' she said. Lazarus could see she looked anything but. She was deathly pale, like all the blood had drained from her, and she was shaking. 'But I feel sick and my head's banging like mad. What happened?'

Her description of how she was feeling reminded Lazarus of exactly how he'd felt, not just when Red had turned up, but the moment he'd seen that arm push through the tear and grab Clair. He wondered if Clair had felt something because she'd been the cause of the hole being opened, willing or not. Or was it because she'd been touched by one of the Dead?

'I need to go home,' said Clair.

'You look like you need to go to hospital,' said Craig. 'You look like hell.'

'That's not exactly funny,' said Lazarus, 'but he's got a point.'

Whatever Clair had done, Lazarus could see that it had really affected her. She said she felt sick, but there was something else about her, too. Her eyes looked glazed over, like they couldn't quite focus on what they were seeing, and Clair was shielding them from the light.

'Seeing as I'm a nurse I'll be at the hospital in a few hours anyway,' said Clair, pushing her hair, damp with sweat, from her face and tucking it behind her ears. 'I'll just go home and get some shut-eye to clear my head before the night shift.'

'You sure you're going to be OK?' Lazarus asked again. He wasn't convinced. No one looking the way Clair did, so different to how they'd looked only minutes ago, could ever be described as OK.

Clair gave a tiny nod. 'Look, Lazarus,' she said. 'I'm sorry about whatever that was. I . . . I can't explain it. I've no idea what happened.'

Clair paused, took a deep breath, and when she stared back at Lazarus he saw fear in her eyes. 'What if I've made things worse?'

Lazarus took a deep breath. He didn't want to think about the possibility of that being true.

'Whatever it was you opened is now closed,' he said. 'Maybe we were lucky.'

Lazarus knew he didn't sound completely convinced.

'What do you mean by making things worse?' asked Craig. 'What actually happened?'

'I need to speak to some people,' said Clair, making her way now past Lazarus and Craig to the door of the lounge. 'See if I can find out more about all this.'

'Like what?' said Craig.

Clair shrugged, then again pushed her hair from her face. Lazarus thought how her skin didn't so much look pale any more, but grey, like ash. He was beginning to wonder just what affect being touched by the Dead could have on a person. Clair wasn't right, that was more than obvious, but if she was off to the hospital anyway, he figured she'd be able to get herself checked out if she still felt rough.

'Look,' said Lazarus, 'whatever happened, well, none of us can explain it, can we? What matters is that it's over. If you can find anything else out, Clair, that's great, but I reckon it's probably best if we all just forget about it, right?'

Clair nodded and said, 'I really am sorry, Lazarus. Nothing like this has ever happened before.'

'Let's hope it doesn't happen again then, eh?' replied Lazarus.

He watched with Craig as Clair shuffled out of the room, heading for the front door. They both heard it shut behind her with a tiny click. In the silence that followed he couldn't shift a sense that whatever Clair had done, accident or not, was going to come back and haunt him.

Lazarus glanced around the room. 'Best tidy up, then,' he said.

'Tidy up?' said Craig after a moment. 'You can't be serious. Not after what we've just seen.'

'I'm totally serious,' said Lazarus. He could hear the anger in his own voice. 'If you hadn't brought Clair over ...'

'And what's that supposed to mean? You saying this was my fault?'

'Well I didn't invite her!'

Lazarus didn't like the way all this had started to dictate

his life. He had to regain control.

'Look, I didn't mean it like that.'

'I know,' said Craig. 'But you're right – maybe I shouldn't have got her to come over. I didn't know anything like this was going to happen.'

'Neither of us did,' said Lazarus. 'And I don't know about you but I want to forget all about it and just get on with having a decent summer. Whatever Dad's involved with, whatever this is all about, he can deal with it. Not my problem.'

'It's going to be pretty hard to forget though, isn't it?' said Craig.

'I guess so,' said Lazarus. 'You still on for that trip to your parents' caravan?'

'Totally,' said Craig, though Lazarus heard the uncertainty in his voice.

'Good,' said Lazarus. Although he was absolutely sure he wanted to bin the last twenty-four hours and get on with his life, he heard his voice falter a little. He coughed and forced a smile. 'I'll go and get a few bin bags and stuff and we can make a start on sorting all this out.'

As he reached the door, he looked back at his mate. If

he couldn't be honest with Craig, what was the point in being mates at all?

'One more thing,' he asked. 'You mind staying over tonight?'

'No worries,' nodded Craig. 'I'll give Mum a call, but it'll be fine. Always is.'

'Cool,' said Lazarus. 'It's just that, well, you know, after what's happened . . .'

He didn't want to spell it out. He didn't want to admit he was terrified to be home alone.

'Totally,' said Craig, and pulled out his phone.

After Craig's mum had agreed to the stay-over, they cracked on with clearing up. They didn't make much of a dent, but it was a start. Tomorrow, Lazarus decided, he'd get some stain remover and work on sorting out the blood. But until then, he was happy that at least they'd cleared up some of the mess and broken glass.

With pizza delivered, they headed upstairs to scoff the lot in front of the TV in Lazarus's room. But no matter how they tried to distract themselves, neither of them were able to avoid the fact they were both scared.

'You know,' said Craig, finishing off the last piece of pizza without asking if Lazarus wanted any of it, 'we can always go stay at mine if you want. My mum would be more than fine about it.'

'I need to stay here,' said Lazarus.

'Why? You think that weirdo's coming back?'

'Maybe,' said Lazarus. 'Don't know really. I guess I'm just spooked by it all.'

'Thought you said it was down to your dad to deal with it, that you just wanted to forget all about it?'

Lazarus knew Craig was right – he had said that. Felt it even. But something deep down was gnawing at him. And no matter what he thought of his dad, or how rubbish their whole father-son relationship was, he was still his dad and that had to mean something, didn't it?

'Look, let's go to my place,' said Craig. 'It's no bother. Really. Get away from here and you'll feel different.'

Lazarus shook his head. He was staying put, and he knew why. 'It's not just what I saw,' he said. 'It's what Red told me about Dad. I need to be here if he calls, just in case.'

'Just in case of what?' asked Craig. 'Look, I know what

you saw – what happened in the lounge was nuts – but do you really think your dad's got anything to do with it?'

Lazarus didn't have an answer. Not a straight one, anyway. But he knew he was staying because of his dad, and that was a little confusing. Was it because he felt a sense of duty to him? It certainly wasn't love. Couldn't be. Loving Dad would be like giving a hug to a dead fish.

'I've no idea what to think,' he shrugged, unable to make sense of how he was feeling. 'But Red gave me a message, remember? I have to tell Dad someone is trying to get through from here to the Land of the Dead.'

'Do you have any idea how nuts you sound?' asked Craig. 'Say that in a public place and you'll be wearing a very tight jacket and locked up in a nice, comfy cell with no windows.'

'To be honest,' said Lazarus, 'I think I'm more pissed off with Dad for not being around when all this happened than anything else. And I can't believe he left his mobile behind. Shows just how little he cares, doesn't it?'

Craig didn't reply.

'But if he does know whatever the hell that was, has

any idea what's going on, I want to find out first. And I can only do that by being here in case he calls,' Lazarus went on. 'And tomorrow, I figured on having a rummage through his office. Might find some clue as to where he is. If I can find an hotel address or something at least I can give him a call.'

Lazarus fell silent. If he was honest with himself, he wasn't exactly sure why he wasn't just heading off to stay at Craig's. Perhaps it was in case that stranger turned up again. Perhaps it was in case his dad called. Or was it just that he was curious? He had a suspicion it was more of the last than anything else.

It was just gone one in the morning when Lazarus stirred. He was thirsty as hell and knew he'd never get back to sleep unless he downed a glass of water first.

He stumbled across the room to the bedroom door, stepping over Craig on the way, his foot only narrowly missing the open pizza box.

The house was cool and silent, and Lazarus could see his breath in the air. With a shiver, he hurried down to the kitchen, where he poured a pint-sized glass of water from a bottle in the fridge. He then headed back up to his room.

Walking up the stairs, Lazarus noticed that the house seemed blacker. He checked the window at the halfway landing. It was darker outside. He guessed that, once again, the summer wasn't doing its job properly and that it would soon be raining. At the top of the stairs he turned right to head back to his room. He was exhausted and just wanted to pass out.

As Lazarus went to push open his bedroom door, he heard the sound of breath being exhaled. At first, he thought it was Craig just about to start snoring. But then he heard it again and realised that it hadn't come from inside the room at all, but from behind him.

From the stairs.

11
RUSTY SWORD

Lazarus felt a shiver of ice race up his back, the hair on his neck not so much standing on end as shrivelling up under the freeze that had stolen into the night.

The sound of the breath came again, and this time Lazarus was sure he didn't just hear it. He felt it too. He didn't want to turn around. He didn't want to face who or whatever it was that owned that breath. Not after the night before. Not after Red and those creatures . . .

Another breath. Lazarus tried to move. It was like the air around him had turned sluggish, as though he were trying to move through deep water. But eventually he managed to turn from his door, pushing the fear deep down inside himself, utterly determined to face whatever the hell else had appeared in his house.

Waiting for the darkness to clear, for his eyes to focus,

the only sound Lazarus could hear was his heart once again thumping a beat that was more run-away than look-see.

Then, almost too quickly, the darkness took shape. Lazarus's eyes zoned in on what was with him on the landing.

It was perched on the post at the top of the banisters: a crouched figure, arms resting over its knees, head down. The long brown coat it was wearing almost touched the floor, and made the figure look like a knackered crow sitting on a tree stump. It looked up. With its face held in shadow, Lazarus couldn't make out any features, but he knew it was staring at him. He also knew that it was blocking the only exit.

Moonlight broke through the window on the landing. It fell on the figure. Lazarus realised he'd seen this person before: first outside the front of the house, then in his dad's study, jumping out through the window. Now he or she was here, almost floating above the stairs. In one hand was a sword: rusty, jagged and huge. In the other, a wine bottle.

Lazarus felt the glass slip from his hand. It seemed to

take an age to reach the floor. When it did, the water splashed out across the carpet, over his feet. The glass itself stood upright for a second or two longer than it should have, then toppled softly on to the carpet. Lazarus opened his mouth to speak, but his voice felt trapped. He tried to back off. All he managed to do was shuffle away, his feet refusing to move more than a few centimetres.

Lazarus's mind was spinning. Why was this person here? What did they want? What had they been doing in Dad's study? But the one thing that bothered him more than anything was this: just how the hell were they balancing on the banisters like that?

The figure jumped soundlessly to the floor, landing with the grace and silence of a feather, then stretched tall and walked towards Lazarus, its sword hanging down and scraping a thin line across the carpet. It lifted the wine bottle and gulped and gulped. Then tossed the empty bottle to one side before wiping its mouth with its sleeve.

Lazarus had become utterly detached from his body. He was helpless as the figure drew closer.

He was going to die.

This person, this creepy freak was going to skewer him

like a pig on a spit. Where was Craig, for God's sake? Why couldn't he hear what was happening?

Lazarus didn't turn away when the figure stopped in front of him. He wasn't going to give it the satisfaction of seeing his fear.

The figure spoke.

'Lazarus, my name is Arielle.'

Lazarus was stunned. The voice was female. He had never heard a voice like it. It seemed to echo, like this Arielle was talking in a church. It sounded impossibly old, yet somehow young at the same time. It was freaky weird, almost hypnotising to listen to.

'I am an old friend of Tobias, your father,' said Arielle. 'I need to speak with him urgently. I have not heard from him for a month now. Where is he?'

'An old friend?' Lazarus couldn't believe what he was hearing. 'Dad doesn't have any friends, then two show up within hours of each other? Who the hell are you? How do you know Dad? I've never heard of you or seen you before!' Another question struck him. 'And if you are an "old friend", why did you break into his office?'

Lazarus was beginning to tire of all this insanity. From

Red turning up, to Clair doing her thing downstairs and re-opening the rip, to this Arielle with her weird-as midnight balancing trick, he was halfway to just packing up. None of it made sense, and it seemed that sticking around was just making it worse.

'Your father and I had an . . . appointment,' continued Arielle, still hidden in the shadows of the hallway. It sounded, thought Lazarus, like she was trying to choose the right words, like she was disguising something. 'But he did not appear. And you said another old friend turned up? Who?'

When Lazarus answered, his voice hissed like a snake. 'Where is Dad? He left his phone behind, and that doesn't make any sense at all, not if I'm supposed to be able to call him in case of emergency, does it? What's going on? Why do you need to speak to him? Oh yeah – and why did you nick his diary?'

Adrenaline was in his fingertips. He was in full on fight-or-flight mode. And Lazarus always stayed for the fight.

'I can explain . . .'

'I bet you can,' spat Lazarus, clenching his fists.

'Lazarus, I don't have time for this,' Arielle said. 'Your father – where is he? And you haven't answered my other question – who was this other old friend?'

'Dad's away on business!' Lazarus shouted, deciding to keep anything to do with Red out of the conversation. 'That's all I know because that's all he ever tells me.'

'You have a contact number?'

'Yeah,' snapped Lazarus, 'but like I said, it's no bloody use, seeing as Dad left his phone at home in his desk!'

'You have no way of contacting your father? No way at all?'

'None,' said Lazarus, glancing back at his room, still unable to work out why Craig couldn't hear what was going on. 'I don't even know where he is.'

'That makes two of us,' said Arielle, turning away from Lazarus and back to the stairs. 'And that's very wrong indeed.'

Lazarus watched as the woman walked away from him into the moonlight now hanging in through the window. At last he was able to see her. She was tall, thin, and seemed to glide rather than move across the floor.

Her hair was black and long, but it didn't look well cared for. It was matted and knotted and pulled back into a loose plait. Her eyes were sunken and her face, though not unattractive, was furrowed with stress, strong cheekbones standing out in an elf-like face. And her skin, Lazarus saw, was milky white, like it had never seen the sun, not even for a day.

Through his fear, Lazarus was intrigued. Why would his dad, the quiet mouse of a man who apparently had no friends outside of his clocks, hang out with this weirdly dressed woman?

'Look,' said Arielle.

A book lay in her hand. Lazarus recognised it straight away. It was his dad's work diary. Arielle flicked through the pages, then pointed to a day circled in blue pen.

'This is when I was supposed to meet him,' she said. 'But Tobias never turned up. Why not?'

'I'm not my father's keeper,' snapped Lazarus. 'Anyway, how do I know you're not lying? How do I know you're not after him for some other reason?'

Lazarus noticed a flicker of a smile on Arielle's face. What on earth had he just said that was so funny?

'I assure you,' said Arielle, 'I have only his best interests at heart.'

'And so do I,' snarled Lazarus.

He wasn't sure why he was so angry. It wasn't as though he really cared that much for his dad, was it?

For a moment neither spoke. Lazarus watched Arielle put his dad's diary away, then pull something else from an inside pocket and lift it to her mouth. It caught the moonlight as she drank. It was a large hip-flask.

Great, Lazarus thought. An alcoholic. His dad didn't drink a drop, was teetotal, so what was he doing getting mixed up with this wino?

Arielle let the flask drop and wiped her mouth on her sleeve. 'I think your father is in trouble,' she said, 'the like of which you couldn't possibly imagine.'

Lazarus almost laughed. 'Oh, I think I've a fair idea,' he said.

'He is responsible for something,' continued Arielle. 'And I need to make sure he hasn't turned from this responsibility.'

Lazarus walked towards Arielle, feeling more confident now that she sounded about as confused as he was.

'You're speaking in riddles,' he said. 'My dad advises banks and private companies and rich gits on how best to make sure their money's safe. What's he got to do with you?'

Before Arielle had a chance to answer, Lazarus was speaking again, unable to stop himself.

'You're going to start talking about veils and the land of the Dead and how the Dead are coming aren't you? Well, however Dad's involved, just leave me out of it, OK? It's not my problem!'

There was a sudden blur of movement. Lazarus yelled. Arielle had grabbed his right arm, swung him round, and pinned him to the wall with a strength that shocked him, her right hand gripping his throat, pushing his head back. The woman was skinny, fragile-looking. Lazarus would've been surprised if she'd have been able to push him over, never mind slam him against a wall.

Arielle shoved her left hand firmly on Lazarus's chest, and he felt very aware of the sword; it was now way too close for comfort. He smelt the taint of alcohol on her breath as she leant in. Her voice, still and quiet, asked, 'How do you know about the land of the Dead? Who told you? Your father? It was not your time to know – not yet! He knows that!'

Lazarus felt Arielle's grip tighten. 'No!' he choked. 'Dad doesn't say anything to me about anything. It was another bloke. Called himself Red. Looked like he'd been in a road accident.'

'Red was here? He was the other old friend?'

Lazarus nodded.

'When?'

Lazarus couldn't be bothered to hold anything back. What was the point? He wasn't going to argue with a woman boozed up and holding a sword to his neck. So he told Arielle everything. It sounded like total gibberish, but he was beyond caring. When he finished speaking, Arielle eased her grip and let him go. Lazarus staggered back.

'What's this all about?' he croaked, rubbing his neck. 'If you know something, if you know what's going on, then tell me. Is Dad in danger? Am I?'

'Your father has disappeared, Lazarus,' Arielle said. 'And Red is not the only one to have noticed that the Dead are stirring. We all did. And trust me when I say that this is bad.'

'What do you mean by we?' said Lazarus. 'Who is Red? Who are you?'

Something about the look Arielle gave Lazarus made him more uneasy than ever.

'Keepers do not disappear, Lazarus,' said Arielle, taking a step forward, her voice soft and sad. 'I have no choice but to assume the worst.'

'Assume what?' said Lazarus, eyes drawn again to Arielle's sword as he backed away, wondering what Arielle meant by keepers.

'I'm sorry, Lazarus,' said Arielle and she took another slow, deep slug from her hip flask before slotting it back inside her coat. 'What I'm about to do ... what I *have* to do ...'

Lazarus heard sadness in her voice. It didn't reassure him. 'Where's Dad?' he pleaded.

Arielle's eyes were on him. 'Only a Keeper can keep the Dead at bay, Lazarus, and seal the veil should it be broken. Close it ...'

'You're sounding like Red,' Lazarus replied, tears threatening to burst from his eyes now. 'But it still doesn't mean anything to me! I don't know what you're talking about! I really don't!'

Lazarus saw just how tired she looked. He also saw a determination that made him realise, were he to even think about trying to escape, she'd be on him in seconds.

He was screwed.

'Lazarus,' said Arielle, moving closer still and sheathing the sword, 'it should not happen like this . . . I am sorry, but I have no choice . . . I would ask you to trust me, but with what I'm about to do, it is impossible. But you will understand eventually. You have to.'

Frozen with fear, Lazarus watched Arielle reach into her coat, pull out an enormous revolver and push it into his chest.

He felt the muzzle of the barrel stab into him, pinch flesh.

No time to react.

'I'm sorry,' Arielle whispered.

In the darkness behind her, Lazarus was sure he saw the grey silhouette of wings silently unfold.

Then she pulled the trigger.

12

✦ TORN TO SHREDS ✦

The first thing Lazarus saw was his own body, still dressed in the pyjama bottoms he always wore, lying on a hospital gurney. Wires and tubes were attached to it. A heart monitor was to one side sending out a weak erratic beep.

For a split second he thought he was awake during an operation, staring up at a mirror, which was why he could see his body and all the medical machinery attached to it.

Then the truth of the moment blasted into Lazarus with the force of a plutonium warhead. He wasn't looking up at all.

He was looking down.

He tried to move, thrashed his arms and legs about, but his body didn't move. It just lay there beneath him, still and pale except for the very obvious and bloody bullet wound in his chest.

Lazarus remembered Arielle, remembered the gun.

He tore at himself, pulled at his hair, anything to bring him out of this awful nightmare. Nothing worked. Was he dead? He couldn't be; dead was dead, wasn't it? That's what he'd always thought, always believed. One life and all that. No forever after. But if that was the case, how could he possibly explain this?

As philosophical questions threatened to drown him, a calm swept over Lazarus. The panic he'd felt at seeing his own body beneath him dissolved in an instant. And, most strange of all, he felt peaceful.

Yes, he realised, *I'm dead. And you know what? It's not that bad.*

Watching his body, listening to the heart monitor and his own breathing, Lazarus thought about what Craig would have to say. Was it one of those NDEs he was always on about: a Near Death Experience? He laughed. Craig would go nuts if he ever got the chance to tell him about this.

The door to the room opened. When Lazarus saw who

had just walked in, his laughter died and he felt cold.

It was Arielle.

The woman who'd shot him strolled over to the operating table to stand at the top of the bed near his head. Lazarus yelled, screamed for help, for someone to come in and get this murdering nutjob away from his body, but it did no good – no one could hear him, and even if they had, he guessed they wouldn't have been able to see him.

He was a ghost.

Arielle reached into her coat. Lazarus saw her pull out the large hip-flask he'd seen her drink from just moments before she'd shot him. He felt his whole spirit crawl as he remembered the smell of alcohol on her breath when he'd been pushed up against the wall.

Arielle looked up at Lazarus and nodded, raised the flask to him in a faint salute.

She can see me! realised Lazarus as she drank. *Oh God . . .* Questions thumped into his mind like torpedoes. *What is she here for? To make sure I'm dead? Is that it? The sick bitch!* He had never felt so helpless in his whole life.

Arielle winked and turned back to Lazarus's body. She tucked her flask away and placed her hands directly over the bullet wound. Lazarus heard her voice. It slipped up to him like steam from a kettle. He tried to grasp the words, work out what Arielle wanted, what she was doing, but whatever language Arielle was speaking it certainly wasn't English. It had a musical edge to it, and a rhythm that seemed to spin the words along so they danced into each other.

Lazarus felt warmth spreading from his chest across his body. It didn't burn, just tingled, like someone had rested a hot-water bottle on his chest. A moment or so later, Arielle slipped her hands away. Lazarus watched as she pulled what looked like an envelope from a pocket and slipped it under his pillow.

What had she done? And why did Lazarus now feel strangely drawn to his body, like he wanted to jump right back into it? He noticed another sound: a distinct, clear, regular beep. It was the heart monitor. But it was no longer erratic and weak; it was strong. And his chest wound looked different, Lazarus thought: less bruised, less life-threatening.

Lazarus could feel himself sinking now, slipping through the air down towards his body. Arielle, the woman who'd shot him, had healed him. At least, that was the only thing that could explain what had happened. How? Why? And was there any way his life could get weirder?

A sound made Lazarus turn. Arielle was back in the room. She flicked something into the air. Lazarus saw it clear as day – a bullet. Somehow, she had removed it from his chest.

Arielle pushed open the door and slipped silently away.

The sound of the gunshot exploded in Lazarus's mind like a land mine. He sat bolt upright, back in his body again, heart crashing against his ribs, breathing hard and fast, his hands grabbing at his chest. It was covered in bandages.

He rubbed his eyes, shook his head, pushed the sound of the bullet as far away as he could. Then he looked around.

The room was white. Wires and tubes led into and out of his body. A heart monitor beeped to one side. He lay there for a minute, not moving, half expecting something bad to happen. But nothing did.

His body ached, but that hardly surprised him,

considering everything that had taken place over the past forty-eight hours. He tried not to think about it all, blocked it out, thought of something else. It didn't work. Not even a little.

Lazarus grabbed hold of his pillow and pulled it over his face. As he did so, he felt something hard knock against the back of his head. He twisted round to see a brown envelope with a number scrawled on it lying underneath his pillow. He remembered Arielle, remembered her putting something under his pillow before she left.

He reached for it and tipped the contents out on to the bed. It was an old mobile phone that looked like it had been run over a few times, then thrown off a cliff.

Lazarus hammered in the number from the envelope. The voice that answered chilled him.

'Lazarus.'

Arielle . . .

'I'll pick you up in the morning. We have a lot to talk about.'

'That's an understatement!' hissed Lazarus. 'You shot me! You tried to bloody murder me!'

He heard a shuffle of laughter down the line.

'If it's any consolation,' said Arielle, 'I did the same to your dad.'

The line was dead before Lazarus had a chance to react. He sat there for a moment staring at the phone. Then he threw the thing across the room. It slammed into the wall, fell to the floor and let out a pathetic beep.

I did the same to your dad . . .

Lazarus felt suddenly very betrayed. His dad was involved with – was to blame for – everything that had happened to him these past two days. And yet he'd never told him, never warned him. Just left him to deal with it on his own. Rage and confusion twisted his stomach.

Some father.

Lazarus heard the door of the room slide open. He looked up to see a nurse walk into the room. She was carrying a cloth-covered tray and smiling. He smiled back, then realised he knew her. It was Clair. She'd mentioned that she worked at the hospital – but he hadn't been prepared to see her so soon after what had happened. And she looked so different in her uniform, like another person almost; a stranger. She'd mentioned something about going to try and find out more about what had happened.

Was that why she was here, to give him some answers?

'Hi,' he said, his voice dry, croaky. 'How you doing?'

Clair didn't reply. Instead, she placed the tray on the bedside table, then walked over to the curtains, her shoes clicking lightly on the floor, and pulled them shut.

Seeing Clair made Lazarus realise just how sore his whole body felt. He hoped that whatever she was about to give him, it involved serious pain relief and sleep, and if it managed to erase the last two days from his memory as well, all the better. Being in that room was nice. He felt comfy. And it was quiet. He wanted to forget about everything. Especially his dad.

But he couldn't. Red had turned up and his life had been torn to shreds. All sense and normality had been blown apart. He'd seen things that terrified him beyond anything he could have ever imagined. He'd seen the Dead.

A flashback to that night scorched through Lazarus. It was all he could do not to panic and yell out. He tried to focus on Clair, on what she was doing in the room, but it was difficult. Fear was taking hold again.

In his mind, Lazarus was back in his lounge. The Dead

were coming, and Lazarus had seen them: horrifying almost-humans with a hunger in their eyes that wanted to devour him on the spot. All that he'd seen and experienced and heard and smelt was real; every moment, every terror, right down to being shot and being here.

No. He didn't want to think about that.

Trying to get a grip, Lazarus watched Clair glide across the room and lock the door. That sound, the feel of the room, made him feel secure. He allowed his eyes to close, his body to relax.

His mind, though, refused to have anything to do with such an idea. It wanted answers, and it wanted them right now. But where was he supposed to begin? The only one who would have any answers was his dad. And he was the one person Lazarus hadn't a clue how to find.

Thinking all this made his brain hurt. Lazarus bunched his fists into his eyes. Sparks burst in the dark behind his eyelids. When he opened them again, he felt his head spin. He needed fresh air, saw that the window was open, and made to climb out of bed to walk over.

Clair was suddenly, silently, at his side, easing him back into bed, her soft voice telling him everything was OK, that he would be better to lie down, to let himself recover. He resisted, heard himself mutter something about feeling dizzy, but his voice didn't sound quite right. He just let Clair lie him back down, cover him up, tuck him in nice and tight.

Too tight.

Lazarus tried to move and found it difficult. The sheets were so snug around him that he felt stuck to the bed. He struggled a little, but he just didn't seem to have the energy. Clair was being so nice, wasn't she? Making him feel so rested, so in need of recovery that he thought that yes she had a very good point, and that lying down was a much better idea.

As his head touched the pillow, he looked over at her. She was still busy with his bed sheets, straightening them out, tucking them in even further.

Well, there's no moving now, he thought, and allowed his eyes to slip shut. Sleep was coming, he could tell, and it was so totally what he needed. Lots and lots of sleep, the perfect cure.

But something made Lazarus stop. He opened his eyes again. What was it that was bothering him suddenly?

He looked around the room, at the window, at Clair. It wasn't anything he could see. No, it was something else, something faint, difficult to notice. So faint he'd almost missed it. But it was there. And when he realised when he'd last experienced it, he felt the blood drain from his face.

It was the smell.

And it was coming from Clair.

13
BLOODSHOT EYES

Lazarus struggled against the sheets, but he was stuck tight like a fly in a web. Clair was standing at the side of his bed. She looked so normal, so wonderfully *human*. So why the smell? Why was it coming from her?

Lazarus remembered coming back into the lounge to find Clair opening the rip, and one of the Dead pushing through. He remembered how it had grabbed her, how he'd had to slam the thing with a plank of wood hard enough to knock them both to the ground to make it let go. What the hell had it done to her?

Clair's head snapped round so hard to face him that Lazarus winced, half expecting the force of the movement to break her neck.

'I have a message, Lazarus.'

Her voice sounded odd, thought Lazarus, like it

was stretched and twisted.

'We have your father now. Do not follow him. Do not stand in our way!'

Lazarus knew she was talking about the Dead. He also knew that it wasn't Clair who was talking, but something else. Arielle had said something about his dad being lost, just before she'd shot him. But what did she mean?

Even if it was the last thing he wanted to do, not least because it probably involved actually helping his dad, Lazarus understood at last that he had to get to the bottom of what was going on. It scared the hell out of him, but he had no choice.

The world went black. Not like the lights had gone out, not like someone had shut the curtains, but like the world beyond that one hospital room had been erased. Lazarus had a horrible feeling that whatever happened now in that room, no one outside it would be any the wiser. Not until it was over.

Lazarus struggled again, pushed and pulled his body, but the sheets weren't about to give. He looked back up at Clair. She was still staring at him, her bloodshot eyes wide open, like they were about to burst out of her skull. Her skin looked strangely taut, like it had shrunk a little and was being pulled horribly across her bones. But why was she still here? Hadn't she given him a message? What else did she want?

What Clair did next burned itself into Lazarus's mind. She rammed her hands into her mouth, gripped her cheeks and stretched her mouth impossibly wide, pulling bloody lacerations across her skin, like she was trying to wrench her face off.

Then she screamed.

That awful sound drilled right through Lazarus. He struggled, his skin wet and slick with sweat, but still the sheets wouldn't give. And Clair was drawing closer now, her mouth getting wider and wider.

The sheets gave way. Lazarus was able to move. Desperately, he pushed himself further up the bed. Pictures were bursting through his brain; images of things in agony being tormented by God knows what, trapped somewhere beyond imagination, the place he'd glimpsed on the night he'd found Red in the lounge. Around him Lazarus felt like the room was crumbling, the walls falling apart, mortar turning to dust, bricks exploding, the whole place getting sucked into nothingness.

The screaming stopped.

Lazarus was now at the top of the bed, no longer trapped, his breathing hard and fast. Clair followed, pushed her face up to him, forced him down on to his mattress. Her face pulled out into an awful, wide-eyed grin. 'All hope is lost, Lazarus . . .'

Lazarus lashed out, but she simply side-stepped. The force of his movement sent him sprawling forward. Clair followed, spoke again.

'You cannot imagine how we have suffered . . .'

Lazarus tumbled off the bed and landed on the floor hard enough to wind him.

'No hope, Lazarus. Just an unquenched thirst to live again. Can you imagine what that's like?'

Clair was stooping over him, her body at a horrible angle.

'We have waited so long. We needed your father. Now everything is in place. Now is the time of the Dead, Lazarus!'

Then she screamed again, that awful sound forcing him to cover his hands over his ears and crawl across the floor.

But as he moved, she simply stayed with him, not even stopping for a breath. Lazarus drew his knees up to his chest and pushed his face to the floor, the cold tiles against his sweating forehead. But it was no good. He had to do something, anything, to make her stop—

Clair stood up suddenly and turned towards the door, like she was making to leave. But something had snapped inside Lazarus. With a crazed yell that felt like it was ripping his heart out, he struck wildly at her. He didn't know what he was doing, wasn't thinking. Something deep down inside him was now telling him what to do.

The movement caught Clair by surprise and she didn't dodge quickly enough; Lazarus's arm made contact with the side of her head and she fell hard to the floor. He felt the sting of the contact burst up his arm, but it wasn't just pain that he felt. His hand seemed stuck to her, glued to her skin, and he couldn't pull it away.

His vision swirled and the room felt suddenly icy cold – he could see his own breath. Something like an electric shock thumped through him, his skin turned to goosebumps, and then it was as though all of his senses had cranked up to ten. He couldn't just hear Clair breathing, but her blood pumping through her veins, the muscles in her eyes trying to focus. And that faint smell, the one that had reminded him of Red, was now strong enough to burn his nostrils.

Lazarus tried again to pull away, yanking at his hand, but it did no good. He glanced up at Clair and gasped. Superimposed over her, he could now see the image of something else, a dark and twisted being, broken and vile: the Dead that had climbed through the portal and sunk its fingers into Clair's skin. Somehow it had become a part of her, pushed its way into her body. But it didn't look happy. It looked like it was doing all it could to get away from his touch and maintain control of Clair.

Clair screamed and Lazarus heard her real voice this time, knew she was fighting against the Dead inside her. But it was obvious to him that she didn't have the strength. She reached for the tray she had brought in, threw off the cover, and pulled out a spike. Lazarus stared at the weapon. He knew now he wasn't fighting Clair but the Dead.

He backed off as Clair raised the spike to plunge it into him. It was a rusty thing with three jagged edges. The handle was a twist of metal thorns that cut into Clair's hand, making her hand burst into a bloody glove. Lazarus felt the contact break between his hand and Clair. He scrabbled away on his back as she brought the spike down. It drove hard into the floor, burying deep.

With inhuman strength, Clair ripped it out. She dived at Lazarus, but he caught her with his feet and kicked out, sending her sailing through the air with such force that when she smacked into the wall, plaster and tiles fell to the floor around her. Lazarus was shocked. He'd just been shot, hadn't he? So how had he recovered so quickly? Just what the hell had Arielle done to him?

He wasn't given time to think as Clair jumped back to her feet and dashed across the floor. Instinct took over as she heaved the spike towards Lazarus a second time. He caught her hand, but the spike slashed him across the chest. It felt like it was pulling the blood from him as it cut into his skin. The reek of burning hit him. Beneath his grip on Clair's wrist, her skin was starting to smoulder and smoke and blister.

The struggle between them became desperate. Lazarus could still see the creature inside Clair, using her as a puppet. They rolled across the floor, crashing into the bed, tearing down the curtain that surrounded it, ripping wires from the walls.

Lazarus's hand came away from Clair's wrist. Then, not knowing what he was doing, he jumped to his feet and gripped her head tight between his palms.

Clair thrashed about violently, her body bucking and shaking, but Lazarus wasn't about to let go. As he held on, something black like pitch started to spill from her eyes and ooze from her mouth. Lazarus felt himself starting to retch but he hung on. Clair thrashed even more. At last Lazarus let go, and she slammed into the floor face first.

For a moment, the room was silent. Clair wasn't moving. Lazarus thought she was dead.

Then, from her chest, something terrible started to push its way out.

14
AGONISING HOWL

A hand came out first, its skin like a plucked chicken, pale and waxy. Then came the arm, blistered and wet. Thin blue veins bubbled and burst across its skin, leaking blood and pus over the floor.

Lazarus backed off, but kept watching as the creature slipped from Clair's body bit by bit. As it emerged further the arm soon led to a shoulder; then the other arm was free. Eventually he saw the head. Its eyes, black and hollow, bled down its cheeks, the skin of its face translucent. The inside of its mouth was black. The creature looked up at Lazarus and grinned.

Suddenly it was free of Clair's body and lying on the floor, its eyes pinned to Lazarus. He glanced back at Clair and was amazed to see that not only she unharmed by this thing, and by the struggle he'd had with her himself, she was breathing as well.

The sound of nails scratching across the floor brought Lazarus back to the creature. It was still crawling slowly towards him, pulling itself along by its fingers. Closer and closer it got until it reached out with its right hand.

Lazarus saw the spike at Clair's side. In a moment of clarity he jumped up, grabbed the cloth Clair had used to cover the tray, wrapped it round his hand and picked up the spike. It bit into his skin, but didn't puncture it.

The creature tried to pull itself round to look at him, but it wasn't quick enough. Lazarus drove the spike into it, pinned it to the floor. It squealed. It pulled at the spike. But it was held fast. The more it struggled, the more it screamed and the more it tore itself – great deep bloody rips spreading from the immovable spike. With a final gut-wrenching screech its skin liquefied and it dissolved to nothing, its agonising howl fading into the walls.

Lazarus felt exhausted and in shock. He dragged himself over to check Clair, his eyes snapping back to the spike jabbed into the floor, an oily slick steaming about it.

Clair was still breathing. Despite everything, she looked peaceful. What had he done? Lazarus looked back at the spike. Somehow, by touch alone, he'd pulled that creature out of Clair. And then he'd driven the spike into it with such force that it had pierced the floor and destroyed the creature. Lazarus remembered what Red had said about not being able to kill the Dead, how they took centuries to get strong again. Wherever that thing now was, he thought to himself, more than a little relieved, he'd certainly never be seeing it again in his lifetime.

A memory charged through Lazarus's mind, bringing him round to where he was and what he was going to do now – it was the conversation he'd had with Arielle before Clair had turned up – she was coming for him in the morning.

I've got to get the hell out of here . . .

He needed Craig.

Lazarus spun round on his knees, looking for the phone Arielle had left for him. He spotted it over by the wall, slid across the floor, picked it up.

God, I hope you're working . . .

He flicked the phone open. Thankfully, his lobbing it against the wall hadn't totally knackered it. He punched in Craig's number.

'Laz?'

'Craig.'

'What the—'

'No time,' said Lazarus. 'I'm in hospital. I need you to get me out.'

'What happened last night?' Craig demanded. 'Where did you go? I woke up and your bed was empty, you weren't in the house. How can you be in hospital? I've spent the whole day wondering what had happened, where you'd gone . . .'

Lazarus didn't want a long conversation. He could explain everything to Craig later on. Except perhaps for how he'd got to hospital because he hadn't a clue. But for the moment, he just needed out.

'Can you get to the hospital?'

Craig sounded more confused than ever. 'It's the middle of the night, Laz.'

'I asked if you can get here. Can you?'

'I guess,' said Craig. 'Why?'

'Because I'm not sticking around to see just how bad everything can really get,' Lazarus snapped. 'Dad's not been there for me once in my whole life and then he leaves me alone to deal with this while he disappears. Well, he's just going to have to work it all out for himself. It's nothing to do with me.'

'You sure?'

'Totally,' said Lazarus.

'But why do you need me?'

'I need clothes,' said Lazarus. 'I can't walk out of here in my PJs, can I?'

Craig laughed, but it sounded empty.

'I'll get myself out of the ward,' said Lazarus. 'You won't be able to get in as it'll be locked. I'll have to improvise a way to get past the nurses. I'll meet you outside the main entrance.'

'Always said you were a sneaky git,' said Craig.

'So I'll see you in how long?'

Craig was quiet for a moment, then sighed and said, 'I'll be there in thirty, OK?'

Lazarus had to get out and meet Craig before anyone raised the alarm or he met Arielle again. And to do that he had to get out of the ward without being noticed.

Clair was unconscious so he figured she wouldn't be a

problem, at least not for the time being. Then he pulled the spike out of the floor, wrapped it in a strip ripped from a bed sheet, crept up to the door to his room and eased it open.

It was grey in the corridor on the other side. About fifty metres ahead he could see the exit doors. Only problem was getting past the reception desk halfway between him and his way out.

Silently he slipped out through the door, quickly ducking into an alcove to the left of the corridor. Here he found a small sink and a microwave and a couple of almost comfy chairs. It was the nurse's break room, but he didn't have time to hang around for a snack. He peered down the corridor. He could just see the reception desk. Sitting behind it was a nurse about the same age as Clair. She looked tired and bored and was reading a book, occasionally glancing up at the computer screen in front of her, probably checking her emails or on Facebook, thought Lazarus.

Lazarus made a move, slipping out of the break room and down the corridor, past rooms like the one he'd been in himself. Footsteps echoed up ahead and he bumped through the nearest door, his heart doing a drum roll.

The room was dark and the only sounds were that of medical instruments and breathing. The footsteps walked past, but Lazarus didn't feel any sense of relief. Getting out was going to be harder than he realised. He leant against the cool wall in the room, tried to gather his thoughts, come up with something. He needed a way to distract the staff on the ward so that he could make a bolt for it. But how?

Turning to look at the patient in the room, Lazarus was struck by an idea. And it made him grin.

He walked quietly over to the person in the bed. It was a man, but that was about all Lazarus could make out in the gloom. He moved to the head of the bed. There, hanging from the ceiling was a pull cord. The emergency alarm. Pull it and everyone would come running.

And they did.

Lazarus had just enough time to bolt from the room to the one opposite before nurses filled the corridor and piled into the room. He counted to five and then, breathing deep, he ripped the door open and ran.

The corridor felt huge as he pelted down it, his feet flapping on the floor. The doors were in front of him. He punched the door-release button and burst through, checked the signs hanging from the ceiling and a map on the wall, then made off towards the main entrance.

Walking as fast as he could without drawing anyone's attention, Lazarus did his best to ignore the aches in every part of his body. Considering all that had just happened, including being shot by Arielle, he felt ready for anything. Perhaps it was just the adrenaline keeping him on his feet. He didn't care; even if he collapsed in a few minutes' time, it didn't matter, so long as he was somewhere else.

Lazarus pushed through a door and the main exit appeared up ahead. It wasn't far now. Then a call came from behind and Lazarus heard the door open.

'Lazarus!'

Lazarus turned – Clair was right behind him. She looked awful, was leaning against the open door, and was staring at him.

Lazarus wasn't about to wait around to find out if she was going to attack him again. He broke into his best version of a run, hobbling and lurching towards the main exit, trying not to trip over his feet.

Clair called again.

'Wait Lazarus! You have to listen to me! Wait!'

But Lazarus wasn't about to wait. He was out of there. He could hear Clair trying to chase after him. He glanced back and saw that she was dragging herself along the wall, the effort making her cry.

Clair called again. 'They know your weakness, Lazarus! They'll use it against you. Listen to me, for your own sake!'

Lazarus stopped. He was far enough ahead now for Clair not to catch him. The main exit was only a step away. He swung a final look round at Clair.

'I'm not interested!' he shouted. 'I'm out of here for good!'

He slipped forward, pushed open the doors, but as he slipped through, he heard Clair call again.

'It's not just the Dead that are coming, Lazarus ... It's Hell, you hear me? And the Dark will swallow everything in its path!'

But Lazarus didn't give himself time to think about what Clair had said, or what she meant – he was out through the main doors now and breathing fresh air.

The shock of the cold night air made him stumble

across the pavement outside and into the road.

'Lazarus!'

Lazarus looked up, saw Craig racing towards him on his BMX and skid to a halt.

'Nice outfit,' said Craig.

'Cheers.'

Craig swung a bag off his back. 'Bung this lot on and you'll at least be warm.'

Lazarus opened the bag. It was stuffed with jeans, T-shirt, fleece jacket and some knackered trainers.

'Remember,' said Craig, 'fashion isn't everything.'

Two minutes later and Lazarus was dressed.

'So what now?' asked Craig. 'Down to the coast and across the Channel to France?'

Lazarus laughed. It felt good. 'Let's just get back to yours and go from there,' he said. 'I need to work out just what on earth's going on before we do anything.'

'Hop on then,' said Craig, nodding at the pegs sticking out of the axle of his rear wheel.

Lazarus went behind Craig, put his hands on Craig's shoulders and placed a foot on one of the pegs.

A horn blared, an engine roared and Lazarus whipped

round to see a huge, mean-looking four-wheel drive charge down the road, tyres skidding the thing to a halt in front of them.

The passenger door flew open. Arielle was in the driving seat.

15

☠☠ TERRIFYING SPEED ☠☠

'Move!' yelled Lazarus. 'That crazy bitch shot me and put me in the hospital!'

Craig hesitated. 'Shot you? Seriously?'

'Just pedal!' said Lazarus.

'No way can we outrun that,' said Craig, glancing at the truck. 'And who's to say she won't just run us off the road?'

'Just go!' screamed Lazarus, and punched Craig in the back. 'Stick to the pavements, use back streets – anything – just get us away from her!'

Craig didn't waste another second. With a push they were off.

Lazarus, gripping Craig's shoulders, held himself low to avoid causing too much drag through the wind. Craig swept them out of the hospital car park, skipped on to a pavement then slipped down an alley.

'Where's this go?' asked Lazarus, lowering himself to Craig's ears to be heard.

'No idea!' replied Craig. 'I'm just winging this, OK? It's not a sightseeing tour!'

The bike bounced down the alley, Craig deftly sweeping it between bins and past a rather startled cat. A road up ahead was getting close fast. Then it disappeared as the end of the alley was blocked by the truck.

'What now?' yelled Craig.

'There!' said Lazarus. 'On the right – open gate. We're going to have to dump the bike!'

'No way!' shouted Craig. 'Mum'll kill me if I do that!'

'And that nutjob down there,' said Lazarus, pointing at Arielle's truck, 'will probably kill us both if we don't get out of here right now!'

But it was too late. Craig hesitated too long and the bike swept past the open gate on a collision course with the truck.

'You idiot!' shouted Lazarus as ahead he saw Arielle climb out of the truck and start to run towards them. 'Now she's going to kill us both!'

Craig slammed on his breaks and Lazarus felt the bike skid left and right as it slowed down. When the bike eventually stopped he jumped off, ready to bolt for the open gate, even if he had to drag Craig with him, kicking and screaming. But as he turned and made to go he saw Arielle sweep up the alley towards them with an impossible speed. It looked like she wasn't even touching the ground, instead just shooting through the air like a bullet.

Craig gasped as Arielle appeared in front of him.

'You have to come with me,' she said. 'Now!'

'How did you do that?' said Craig, staring at Arielle. 'You were down there, but now you're here; how? It's too far, you were too quick!'

'Lazarus?' said Arielle, utterly ignoring Craig.

Lazarus was edging back up the hill. The garden with the open gate was only a few metres away. If he could just get there he'd have a chance . . .

'I told you I'd come in the morning, Lazarus,' said Arielle. 'Why are you making a break now, in the middle of the night? What were you thinking?'

'You shot me!' he shouted, his breath snarling in his throat as he stumbled across the road. 'You bloody well shot me!' He looked down at Craig and said, 'I know this may sound nuts, but that's what she did. And then she pulled the bullet out and then Clair turned up and this Dead thing was in her and . . .'

Lazarus took another step back, tripped, fell. Everything he was saying – thinking – sounded like total nonsense. But he knew that it wasn't.

He heard Arielle speak to Craig.

'You have to trust me,' she said, leaning down next to him. 'Lazarus is more important than you could possibly imagine. We have to get him inside my truck and to safety. Now.'

'No!' Lazarus protested, but for the first time since waking up in hospital, he felt too weak to move.

'Craig,' pleaded Arielle, 'we don't have time for this.'

'Did you shoot him?'

Arielle didn't answer.

'Did you shoot him?'

Craig's voice was laced with fear and confusion.

'Yes,' Arielle answered. 'I shot him. I killed him to save him. To save us all.'

Craig was silent. Lazarus tried to get to his feet, but the

best he could manage was to rise to his knees. He looked up at Arielle. How could he trust her?

'You have to come with me, Lazarus,' she said, moving away from Craig. 'Without your father, you are the only hope we have of stopping the Dead.'

Lazarus went to protest, but didn't have the energy. Then Arielle was next to him and he felt himself being picked up with tremendous ease. A few moments later he was sitting in the vehicle. A seatbelt was clipped round him. He tried to push it away, but he was too weak; his hands, his arms didn't respond.

'Craig?'

Arielle again. Lazarus saw his friend standing up the alley by his bike, Arielle bathed in the headlights of the truck, waiting for him. Craig didn't move. Instead, he just whimpered, 'You shot him . . .'

'Don't do this, Craig . . .' said Arielle, her voice turning to a growl.

Craig didn't listen. Instead, he yelled out hard and loud, 'You shot him!' Then he started shouting. 'Help! Someone, please help!'

Lazarus saw Arielle react, knew he couldn't do anything.

One minute she was in front of the truck, a black shadow bathed in light, the next she was with Craig.

'Get off me!' screamed Craig. 'Leave me alone!'

A thump from the back of the truck made Lazarus turn and he saw Craig tumble in and bang his head in the dark. Then the door was slammed shut and Arielle pulled herself in to the driver's seat. She hit the accelerator, and Lazarus felt himself pushed straight back in his seat. Considering the size of the vehicle, it was charging along at a terrifying speed. The houses soon gave way to fields in a blur of grey and green.

'Where are you taking us?'

'Home,' said Arielle, all the time keeping her eyes on the road ahead as she whipped the vehicle round a sharp corner, sending Lazarus sideways. He heard Craig groan in the back of the truck as he was thrown around in the dark.

'But you shot me!' said Lazarus.

'You'll get over it,' said Arielle. 'Why were you running? You knew I was coming. And you've involved Craig, now. What were you thinking?'

'That I had to get the hell away from you, that's what!'

'This is no time for running, Lazarus,' said Arielle. 'Without your father—'

'Without my father what?' Lazarus butted in. 'Like I've said a thousand times, this is Dad's problem, not mine.'

'But you're already involved,' said Arielle. 'You've never had any choice in the matter. It was only a matter of time – just your time came early, that's all. And it's why I shot you.'

'That makes sense,' Lazarus said sarcastically.

'It will do eventually.'

Lazarus couldn't think of anything else to say. He glanced around the inside of the truck to Craig, who was rubbing his head. *You OK?* he mouthed. Craig nodded.

The truck, Lazarus saw, had been converted into a basic caravanette: a two-burner gas stove with a small oven beneath, a small fridge, a sink, a bed on top of which lay a sleeping bag, and plenty of storage. It wasn't exactly luxury; the mattress of the bed was worn and the décor badly chipped. The small window in the side of the truck was too dirty to see through. And the carpet on the floor had seen better days – not that Lazarus could see much of it. It was covered with neatly lined rows of empty wine bottles.

'Plush,' said Lazarus, turning back to stare out the windscreen. 'Going away for the weekend?'

Arielle ignored Lazarus's sarcasm. 'It's a Land Rover Defender one-thirty done to my own spec,' she said. 'It's not designed for comfort, but it's tough as hell and is just about bombproof.' Then she nodded at Lazarus's lap. 'Where did you get that?'

Lazarus looked down. The spike was still clasped in his hand, all but free of the rags he'd wrapped it in. The sudden realisation and sensation of it in his hand repulsed him, and he dropped it into the foot well.

'What happened, Lazarus?' Arielle asked. 'Tell me.'

Lazarus heard Craig scrabble forward and saw him lean over the front seats.

'It was Clair.' Lazarus sank back into his seat, staring into the darkness beyond the truck. His voice sounded distant, like he was talking from inside a dream. 'She's a nurse, remember?' he added, for Craig's benefit. 'She came in to see me. I thought she was there to check up on me. But she wasn't. There was something inside her. I think it was the Dead that grabbed her back at the house. It cut me with that spike, as a warning maybe.

Then things got out of hand.'

'One of the Dead came after you?' asked Arielle sharply.

Lazarus nodded. 'Clair . . . she, I dunno, said something about the Dead coming. Like Red had said, remember? I told you about that, right?'

Arielle nodded.

'Then Clair started screaming. I grabbed her and I could see that thing inside her. It was like my hands were stuck to her skin. The thing came out. I skewered it with the spike.'

Lazarus trailed off, lost suddenly in flashbacks to the fight.

Arielle swung the truck off the main road and on to a thin country lane. The speed she was doing, Lazarus hoped to God they didn't meet someone coming the other way.

A beep sounded from the back of the truck. Arielle snapped round at the same time as Lazarus and they both saw Craig with a phone to his ear.

16

ᴥ☠☠ ROAD KILL ☠ᴥ

Arielle shouted, 'Don't be a damned fool!'

'But you shot Lazarus!' Craig replied. 'For all I know you're taking off into some wood to make sure we're properly dead. I'm calling the police – they're on the phone now!'

Arielle glanced at Lazarus before spinning the truck round a corner and sending a cloud of gravel and muck over a hedge to scare a few cows, and Craig on to the floor to lose his phone. The look in her eyes made him understand that if she'd wanted them both dead, they would be. And no one would know about it for a very long time. Arielle dropped a gear, then bounced them off the road and along a track sunk deep and quiet in to thick woodland. And when it felt to Lazarus like wherever they were no light would ever get to them, the truck skidded to a halt and the sound of Craig bouncing around in the back stopped dead.

Arielle leapt out of the truck and Lazarus heard the rear door open and Craig dragged out. The door was slammed and she was back in the driver's seat.

Lazarus heard Craig scream as Arielle slipped the truck in to first.

'You can't leave him here.'

'I can do whatever I want to do,' said Arielle and pulled the truck round. Lazarus could now see Craig in front of them. He looked terrified, and the lights from the truck were blinding him.

'Either he comes or I don't cooperate,' said Lazarus.

Arielle didn't listen, just started to edge forward towards Craig. Lazarus was suddenly more than a little afraid for his friend. Was she really going to run him down?

Craig started to back off in to the woods.

'I'm serious,' said Lazarus, and knew he sounded desperate. 'Craig comes or you may as well just kill us both here and now.'

'Don't tempt me, Lazarus,' said Arielle.

'I mean it,' Lazarus replied. 'Either you let Craig back

in or whatever it is you want from me, you ain't going to get!'

Arielle jarred the truck to a halt. For a second that felt to Lazarus like it lasted for a year, she just sat there. Then, without a word, she pulled open her door, strode over to Craig, and dragged him kicking and screaming back to the truck, and opened the rear door.

'Get in.'

Lazarus looked round. 'Just do what she says,' he said. 'Unless you want to be road kill.'

Craig jumped in, Arielle slammed the door. Lazarus didn't know if he felt relieved or not. It didn't matter. He and Craig were alive, and that was at least something.

As Arielle pushed the truck in to the night, no one said a word. But the silence was deafening and when Arielle at last spoke, Lazarus was almost pleased. Almost.

'You need some answers, Lazarus,' she said. It was a statement, not a question.

'No kidding,' replied Lazarus sarcastically.

'What you did to that nurse is called an eviction,' said Arielle. 'The Dead need a body to survive, so when they come through that's all they want. The best way to live again is to sink themselves into a nice fresh body and dump the fragile one they arrived in.'

'I'm guessing that's as horrific as it sounds,' said Craig from the back of the truck.

Arielle nodded. 'If one of the Dead occupy you, they don't kill you, they just lock you away. It's a bit like being trapped in a glass suitcase while someone moves into your house and trashes it.'

Craig fell silent.

'And Lazarus,' said Arielle, 'you're not supposed to know about any of this – not yet, anyway. And Craig's not supposed to know any of it at all. But I'm guessing he knows more than he should already, right?'

Craig said nothing. Lazarus just looked at Arielle and waited for her to speak again.

'It's not my job to tell you any of this,' she said. 'But I guard the Keeper. That's my role. Always has been. So that's how I know your dad, being as that's his job.'

'So the security thing's just a cover?' asked Craig and Lazarus could hear in his voice that he was doing his best to pull himself together and push his fear deep down. It didn't matter – it was just good to have Craig along.

Lazarus was beginning to see that whatever his dad had told him about what he did nine-to-five, well, it wasn't exactly the truth. His dad had a secret life, one he'd never told him about. Lazarus wondered what else he didn't know, what else lay hidden.

'So how do you know Red?' he asked Arielle abruptly.

'We go back a long, long way,' said Arielle.

Lazarus could tell she was hiding something. He didn't like it.

'Just before you shot me,' he said, 'something weird happened, didn't it? To you, I mean – not just the fact that you put a bullet in me.'

Lazarus saw confusion light itself in Arielle's eyes.

'How do you mean?'

'Wings,' said Lazarus. 'I hadn't really thought about it until now. Red had them, and that was mental, trust me.'

'Wings?' said Craig in disbelief. 'Are you serious?'

'And I saw them in the darkness behind you, just before you pulled the trigger,' Lazarus went on, still staring at Arielle. 'I'm right, aren't I?'

'It's not important,' said Arielle.

'Yes it is,' Lazarus replied. 'Red said he was one of the Fallen, whoever they are. Then you turn up with wings as well. So what are you, Arielle?'

For a few moments Arielle gazed out through the windscreen, gripping the steering wheel. At last she turned back to Lazarus.

'If you really do want the truth, then I can only tell you a little.'

Lazarus made to protest but Arielle raised her hand.

'If I tell you everything now, Lazarus, nothing will make sense. We – you – have to take this one step at a time or you'll never learn anything. OK?'

Lazarus nodded.

'Good,' said Arielle.

'I just want to say,' Lazarus put in quickly, 'that whatever weird occult stuff you and Dad are into, that's for you to deal with. I'll help you find Dad, but that's it.'

'There's nothing you or anyone else can do about it,' said Arielle. 'The world needs you.'

Lazarus stared. 'Shut up.'

'I'm not joking,' Arielle responded calmly.

'Then don't come at me with such stupid corny lines,'

said Lazarus. He turned to Craig. 'Can you believe this? The world needs me? I mean, what?'

Craig was silent.

'And,' said Lazarus, on a roll now, 'When's Dad ever helped me? When's he ever been there? I don't see why I should be any different for him, do you?'

'This isn't just about your father,' said Arielle. 'This is about all humanity.'

'There you go again with the lines,' sneered Lazarus.

Arielle turned on him. He saw anger in her eyes.

'Your father's gone, Lazarus! Disappeared. For all we know, he's dead!'

'Dead?'

No matter what he thought of his dad, the sudden thought of him being dead scared Lazarus. He was the only family he had. Without him, that was it. No one. No one at all.

'You say you spoke to Red?'

Lazarus swallowed and nodded.

'He's not been seen for thousands of years, Lazarus,' said Arielle. 'For him to look for your father means things are bad. Really, really bad.'

'This is all to do with him telling me the Dead are coming, isn't it? All that stuff about Dad being the Keeper?'

Arielle nodded.

'Red drew this picture in the lounge,' said Lazarus, thinking back. 'It was two circles, one small one inside a much larger one. He said they were veils or something. Told me to tell Dad what he told me.'

'And what did he tell you?'

'Like I said,' said Lazarus, 'that the Dead are coming. And then he said something about someone trying to push through from his side and that they had to be found and stopped.'

'He said that?' Arielle looked paler than usual. 'But that would mean . . .'

Lazarus snapped round at this. 'You know something, don't you?'

Arielle stayed quiet. Lazarus tried some guess work. He figured he'd seen enough of what was going on to give it a decent shot.

'When Red came through to meet me, he had to force a way through the veil, right?' he said slowly. 'I know that because it really messed him up trying.'

Arielle stared at Lazarus. No emotion, not a flicker.

'The Dead can't do that,' Lazarus went on. 'They need something or someone to open up a way for them. Which is what Clair did, so I'm guessing the veil was weak where Red had come through and it was just bad luck that meant we brought in someone who'd open it again.'

Lazarus thought Arielle looked almost impressed. Feeling more confident, he continued.

'So, if Red thinks someone is trying to push through the veil from this side, then they've got two choices: either find a weak area of the veil and open it, or weaken it themselves. But I don't see how that's possible. If Red found it difficult getting through, what chance would a normal person have?'

'Very good,' said Arielle at last, and Lazarus was sure he saw a shadow of a smile flicker across her face. 'Though you're forgetting the third choice.'

'What third choice?' asked Lazarus.

'A gate,' Arielle answered. 'A gate through the veil from this world to the land of the Dead.'

It was Craig who spoke next.

'You're joking aren't you? A gate? But that's impossible,

surely. For a start, why would such a thing exist? And if it does exist at all, why haven't the Dead just bashed the thing in and flooded through?'

'Craig?' said Lazarus. 'What's it like to actually be in a horror movie for once rather than just watching them?'

Craig thought. 'I miss the popcorn,' he replied.

17

🕱 GREY SPECTRE 🕱

'We don't need to worry about the gate,' said Arielle.

'I'm beginning to think I need to worry about everything,' said Lazarus.

'It was broken up, the pieces lost. Some even think that it never existed in the first place. That it was just a wild idea that sent more than a few people insane in trying to find the thing.'

'Why mention it then?' Lazarus demanded.

'Adds a bit of colour to the story.'

A thought struck Lazarus. He stared into Arielle's eyes.

'You think Dad's gone after the person who's trying to get through the veil, don't you? Wherever they are, that's where we'll find Dad. And that's why you're so worried, because he's gone alone. You're supposed to be with him. So actually, this is all your fault.'

'I have no idea where he is,' Arielle said. 'He just vanished. He's supposed to tell me what he's doing. That's why we have regular meetings. But he didn't show. It is most certainly not my fault!'

Lazarus was rather pleased to see he'd managed to get her a little annoyed. Maybe he'd be able to use that to his advantage later on.

'Dad was anal about everything,' he said. 'He's bound to have a record somewhere in the house of where he's gone. He just couldn't arrange to go off like that without leaving some kind of paper trail. It's not his style.'

'You sound like you know him well,' said Arielle.

'No, I don't,' said Lazarus. 'He's just a creature of habit, that's all. I just live with him. Anyway, none of this is explaining why you shot me, is it?'

'I had to,' said Arielle. 'For someone to become a Keeper, they have to die first. It's my job to arrange that. And to bring them back.'

'But I'm not the Keeper, Dad is!' said Lazarus, his voice rising. 'And there's no way I'm following in his footsteps, you hear? No way at all!'

The only response he got from Arielle was a thin, black smile. She revved the Defender's engine hard. Lazarus grabbed the handle above the door with one hand, the dashboard with his other. Arielle rammed the vehicle into first gear, released the handbrake, and accelerated hard. The engine roared, the sound shattering the peace of the wood and scattering wildlife. Lazarus heard the tyres spin, then the Defender lurched forward down the track through the woods.

The track was narrow, barely wide enough for the vehicle, and Arielle wasn't letting up on the accelerator. The trees were a blur. Craig was bouncing around the back of the truck, finding it impossible to hold on. The wing mirrors were doing well to stay attached, considering the whipping they were getting from branches. The track itself was riddled with potholes. It was all Lazarus could do to keep himself in the cab, never mind in his seat.

Craig, having managed to pull himself forward, shouted, 'Do you always drive like this?'

'No,' called Arielle through a wild grin. 'I usually go faster.'

She dropped a gear, whipped the truck round a sharp

bend, sending the rear spinning out, and sprayed mud, grit and water into the air as the track dropped steeply away from them.

'You're insane!' yelled Lazarus as he felt his stomach disappear like he was on a roller coaster. 'Slow down!'

'I know what I'm doing,' said Arielle.

They hit the bottom of a dip, and bounced back up the other side, the tyres tearing at the track as they climbed a steep hill. Lazarus considered closing his eyes, but decided he'd rather see what was coming and prepare for it than have it turn up as a surprise.

Round another corner they went, then the track was straight. It only made Arielle accelerate even harder. The Defender crashed through a puddle that breached the entire width of the track, then took off moments later as it hit a ridge. That moment of silence, as the vehicle grabbed air for a split second, seemed to last for ages. Then it hammered back to earth and chewed its way forward, ravenous for more.

The track disappeared as Arielle launched them out of the wood. Lazarus was suddenly looking down a normal road. He didn't feel relieved at all. Now on a smooth surface, Arielle was able to go even faster. Lazarus knew the Somerset roads as well as anyone. They had a reputation for killing and maiming.

'Please, slow down,' he begged, as they bounced round a hairpin.

Arielle just looked across at him, her eyes dark. Ahead, a crossroads loomed. She didn't even change gear.

A few minutes later, they were back at Lazarus's house. Craig was pale and shaken, Arielle as inscrutable as ever.

'So, Lazarus?' said Arielle. 'Where do you suggest we start?'

'How should I know?'

'Because you're his son and, like it or not, that means you probably know him better than anyone.'

Lazarus didn't want to admit it, but Arielle had a point.

'We'll start in the office,' he said, striding inside, the front door slamming hard against its hinges behind the others. 'If we're going to find anything about where Dad is, it'll be in there.'

He pushed into the room first. It was cool and smelled

musty, and when he flicked the lights on it felt like he'd walked into a room that hadn't been occupied in years. It had the haunting stillness of a museum.

'You check the bookcases,' Lazarus nodded at Craig. Without even turning to Arielle, he pointed at two large filing cabinets. 'See what you can find in there. I'm checking his desk.'

'Pointless,' said Arielle. 'I went through that myself, remember? All I got was his diary and that was no use at all.'

'You could've missed something,' said Lazarus. 'I mean, you've lost my dad, so I'm not sure I trust your observation skills.'

Arielle didn't reply, but Lazarus saw a faint smile crease her lips. After all that had happened, and the fact that he and Craig were still alive, he was beginning to see that perhaps she was on their side after all. OK, so he didn't quite understand what side that actually was, but she was looking for his dad, seemed more than a little concerned about him, and was asking for their help. It was better than nothing. And a whole world better than being dead. He'd already been that, and it wasn't something he was desperate to be again. ·

For the next half an hour no one spoke. Sitting behind his dad's desk, Lazarus went through every drawer, every file he could find. He'd been right about his dad – definitely anal. He found receipts stretching back years for everything from clothes to car repairs. Why hadn't he thrown them away? They were useless.

Craig didn't fare any better. The books were just Tobias's working library. If there was a book in the world on security or locks or bank safes, then his dad had it. It wasn't something to be proud of.

It was beginning to turn to morning now and a grey light was slipping in through the windows. When the light fell on Arielle, she looked ghostlike: a thin grey spectre in a long brown coat. The silence was broken when she shouted in despair and threw a file across the study.

'You idiot, Tobias! Where have you gone?'

'Something up?' Lazarus asked.

'All of this – it's good,' Arielle snapped, waving a hand around the room. 'Too good. Your father was more than brilliant at what he did, Lazarus. No one would ever have suspected that behind this watertight façade he was also the Keeper.'

Lazarus shook his head, trying to understand. 'So what's the problem?'

'The problem,' said Arielle, 'is that if all of this is anything to go by, the chances of your father leaving any hint of his whereabouts are slim, to say the least. He lived and breathed his cover story. He's spent years hiding the truth. What chance have we got of ever finding it?'

Lazarus shrugged. 'This is where his life was. This room. His work was his life. Well, his work and those stupid clocks you see all round the house. He loved those more than me, I'm sure of it.'

'Clocks?' said Arielle.

Lazarus nodded. 'He was always fiddling with them, making sure they were keeping the correct time. In some ways it's weird him not being here – he's never been away long enough to let them start winding down so much that they stop.'

Arielle walked over to a large clock above a fireplace in the far wall. 'Tobias always was obsessed with keeping the right time,' she said.

'That one doesn't work,' said Lazarus. 'He's had it in his

workshop I don't know how many times and it just won't go. Really pissed Dad off, actually.'

Arielle stood back and Lazarus noticed something. Hadn't there always been an old black vase next to that clock? It wasn't there now. It wasn't important, he thought, the disappearance of an ornament – it just jarred, that was all. His dad was so meticulous about everything, it was hard to work out why it would no longer be there. But then perhaps his dad had just got tired of staring at it and got rid of it. Lazarus had never liked it anyway.

Arielle cut into Lazarus's thoughts. 'Workshop? What workshop?'

'The cellar under the stairs,' said Lazarus. 'Dad does all his dull clock repairing stuff down there. Only went down there once, never went back. Cogs and springs and crap like that just don't do it for me.'

But he was talking to Arielle's back. He chased after her, Craig not far behind, and found her outside the door to the cellar.

'Down here?'

Lazarus nodded and looked at the door. It was an unassuming thing, painted white and pricked here and there with holes from drawing pins. A few Post-it notes were stuck to it in places and occasionally caught the breeze that shifted through the old house uninvited. It was the kind of door behind which you'd expect to find coats and boots and a vacuum cleaner and little else.

'Where's the key?' Arielle demanded.

'No idea,' said Lazarus. 'Dad always had it. It's not like I needed it, is it?'

Arielle stepped back. 'You'd better stand clear,' she said.

Lazarus and Craig didn't get a chance to ask why. Arielle had already raised her right foot and launched it at the door.

18

CANDLE GLOW

The cellar door shattered like ice.

'And just why the hell was that necessary?' sighed Lazarus, having only just managed to duck out of the way of the flying splinters.

Arielle didn't answer. 'Is there a light switch?'

Lazarus pointed inside the door. 'Just there, on the right, from what I remember.'

Arielle reached up and flicked the switch. A bulb zipped into operation. Its dusty glow lit a steep stone staircase that folded out of the darkness and led beneath the house. At the bottom stood another door.

'And your father worked down here?' asked Arielle. 'Seriously?'

'He said he liked the quiet of the place,' Lazarus answered. 'And he had it sorted so that it was at a constant temperature. Something to do with not affecting the workings of the clocks. Can't say I really cared.'

'You know, I've always wanted to go down here,' said Craig, unable to disguise the excitement in his voice.

Lazarus led the way. At the bottom of the stairs he opened the second door. Cool air shifted past them as they stared into a thick darkness.

'No lights?' asked Arielle.

'Guess not,' said Lazarus. Then he remembered. 'No, there wouldn't be. Dad was always buying candles for this place. Said he and the clocks preferred the atmosphere.'

'So where are they then?' asked Arielle.

'Like I said, I've only been down here once,' said Lazarus. 'We'll just have to look for them. They must be here by the door, though.'

'Your dad really is weird, isn't he?' said Craig.

Lazarus turned to the wall and started to feel around for a hole or something where he guessed his dad kept matches and candles. But Craig found them first. Then, with a lit candle, he led the way into the workshop, lighting other candles on the way as they slunk out of the gloom, until the whole room was glowing like the inside of a lantern. It felt more than a little strange to stand for the first time in a room in the house he'd lived in all his life, a room his dad had used almost on a daily basis.

It felt like a tomb, a windowless cave occupied by the corpses of clocks waiting for resurrection. The floor was well-worn flagstones, polished by years of use. A large desk was in the middle of the room, a half-mended clock in the centre, its innards spilled out neatly like a perfect autopsy. A leather chair sat pulled under the desk. One wall of the cellar was given over to shelving; clearly labelled boxes filled the space, each containing spare bits of this and that for repairing timepieces. The wall containing the door was bare but for a jacket on a hook. The wall opposite the shelves was little more than a vast cage holding bottle after bottle of wine, many dust-covered, like they had been asleep for years – and they probably had. The remaining wall, the one opposite the door to the place, held only one thing – a picture of someone Lazarus knew all about but had no memory of. His mum.

'Your dad was obsessed,' said Craig, going over to look at the shelves of clock parts attached to the wall.

Arielle called over from a dark corner of the room, the

cage of wine in front of her. Lazarus turned to see her holding a dusty bottle.

'Tobias was a sly old fox,' she said, a wry smile curling her mouth. 'He's got some seriously rare vintages over here.'

Craig said, 'But I thought your dad didn't drink?'

'Seems a lot of what I thought about my dad is total fiction,' Lazarus replied. He sat down at the desk. Laid out in front of him on an oily rag were a few brass cogs and some other bits and bobs he hadn't a clue about. 'We're not going to find anything down here,' he said to no one in particular. 'It's just clocks, Dad's hobby. That's it. It's pointless.'

'We've nothing else to go on,' said Arielle, replacing the bottle of wine. 'If it's not here, then ...'

'Then what?'

Arielle turned to some books on a shelf and started to flick through.

Lazarus nodded at the shelves on the wall by Craig. 'You OK to look through those?' he sighed. 'Don't ask what we're trying to find. Just if you see something that doesn't fit in a place dedicated to saving clocks, let me know.'

Craig got on with searching. Lazarus turned back to the desk. Apart from the clock pieces, the desktop itself was clear except for a large church candle on one corner at least a foot high. Lazarus leant forward to light it, then moved on to the drawers. Those on the left were filled with yet more receipts, though these were all to do with clocks. They were dated and filed in order and Lazarus was struck with an urge to shuffle them all up. The drawers on the left were empty. The only other drawer was the one in the middle. It was slim and wide and when Lazarus gave it a tug it moved easily, the runners obviously well worn, and slid open to reveal, at last, a little hint of untidiness in his dad's world. Pens jostled for position with broken pencils, a ruler and a small hardback book on basic carpentry skills. A box of paperclips had spilt its contents and a couple of tins of small cigars lay open and half empty. This was another surprise – Lazarus didn't know his dad had ever smoked. The rest of the drawer was given over to a fairly large collection of old moleskin notebooks held together in bundles of three with brown twine.

Lazarus pulled out one of the bundles and started to untie them, expecting to find little more than his dad's notes on repairing clocks. But when he opened the first book and read the first page, he felt a shiver race up his back. He was looking at his dad's personal diaries.

For a few moments he wondered if looking in the diaries was a good idea at all. In them were the thoughts of someone he thought he'd known at least a little about; it turned out that he'd known absolutely nothing. He'd lived a lie and he was angry. Why hadn't his dad trusted him enough to at least give him some idea of all this? He was tempted to burn the books with the candle flame. But curiosity eventually took hold and he opened a diary.

Lazarus had no idea how long he'd been looking at the diary, except that when he looked back up, half the candle had disappeared and what he'd read in the pages of the book had changed everything. Time hadn't just flown, it had dissolved with every word, paragraph and page Lazarus had read.

'Lazarus?'

Lazarus looked up to see Arielle and Craig.

'What is it? What have you found? You've been very quiet.'

Lazarus didn't know where to begin, so pushed the question back. 'What about you?' he asked. 'Anything?'

'Just this,' said Arielle and rested a box of papers on the desk. 'It's all in your dad's handwriting, but it's just research.'

'How do you mean?'

'Notes on the Dead,' explained Arielle. 'He was a thorough man. He's cross-referenced the notes to a pile of books I found over there, some of which are ancient. But it's nothing out of the ordinary, not if you consider what your father actually did. Your dad just wanted to know everything about what he was dealing with, and if that meant finding out how to walk in the land of the Dead to track down a particularly nasty customer, then that's what he'd do.'

'Walk there?' said Lazarus. 'You mean someone living can cross over, too?'

'Even if it is possible,' said Arielle, 'you'd need a damned good disguise. The Dead would be on you like stink.'

'If it's all the same with you,' said Craig, 'I'd prefer to stay here.'

'Anyway Lazarus,' said Arielle, 'what did you find?'

'These,' said Lazarus. He handed the book in his hand to Arielle, then reached for another and gave it to Craig. 'Dad's diaries. His proper ones. He's been keeping them for years. The earliest I've found starts just days after Mum was killed.'

Arielle and Craig opened the books, flicked through the pages.

'And if the person in those books is my dad,' said Lazarus, leaning back in his chair, 'then just who the hell have I been living with all my life?'

'How do you mean?' asked Arielle. 'This is your father's writing. I'd recognise it anywhere.'

'I mean,' said Lazarus, 'that Dad's about as emotional as a bag of chips. He doesn't get excited about anything, show feelings, even to me.' He reached into the desk and pulled out the rest of the diaries, thumping them down on to the desktop. 'So tell me, Arielle, did you know that Dad cries every night thinking about Mum? Because I didn't. And that's weird, isn't it?'

Lazarus could see that Arielle still didn't understand.

'There are poems in here for God's sake,' he said, opening a page to one he'd read a few minutes ago. 'And there's stuff in here about me, too.'

'Like what?' asked Craig.

'Like how proud he is of me and how much he loves me,' said Lazarus. 'Like how life without Mum is unbearable, that he couldn't live without her, that he wanted her back. So why didn't he just tell me face-to-face instead of writing it in a book in a cave, eh?'

'Lazarus,' said Arielle, 'I know this is all a bit of a shock—'

'Can you imagine it?' continued Lazarus. 'There's Dad, dealing with the Dead, sending them back. Then he loses his wife and he's got all this knowledge and power but can't stop her dying, can't bring her back? Seems a bit unfair, don't you think?'

'Lazarus,' said Arielle, her voice calm and measured, 'did you find anything that would tell us where your dad has gone? Anything at all?'

Lazarus picked up one of the bundles of diaries and shook it in front of Arielle's face. 'Gone? He's never been here! Ever! It's like Dad died the day Mum was killed and he's just hidden himself away down in this cave, refusing to get over it and move on. And no one noticed. Not even me!'

'Look, Lazarus,' said Arielle, reaching out a hand to him, 'there's nothing I can say. You dad was always quiet, always kept himself to himself.'

'And stop talking about him in the past tense!' yelled Lazarus, springing up out of the chair, knocking away Arielle's hand. 'He's not dead!'

With a yell, he launched the diaries across the cellar. They slammed into the picture of his mum, shattering the glass.

Silence.

'Feel better?' asked Arielle.

'No,' choked Lazarus. 'All I know is that I've just found out that I have a dad I never knew existed and I'm not about to have him die on me now, all right? Wherever he is, we're going to find him and bring him back.'

'But we still need a clue, Lazarus,' said Arielle. 'Are you sure nothing in those diaries told you where he might have gone?'

Lazarus went to answer – but then he saw something on the wall behind where the picture of his mum had been, something catching the candle light. When he took a closer look, he saw a tiny brass eyelet where a little key would sit.

Arielle stepped forward. 'What is it Lazarus?'

Lazarus didn't answer. Instead he pulled out the key hanging from a chain round his neck, the one his dad had given him.

'Lazarus?'

'A hunch,' said Lazarus and slipped the key in to the hole. He twisted it and a soft thud somewhere behind the walls of the cellar sent a shuffle of dust from the shelves.

'I know I'm going to regret asking this,' said Craig, 'but what the hell was that?'

Lazarus wasn't given a chance to answer as the wall in front of him was suddenly split floor to ceiling by a thin line that coughed dust. Then, with a sound like a mill stone grinding, the wall started to slide open. As the gap widened, Lazarus could see behind it a thick darkness swirling like fog, and wide, shallow steps disappeared down in to it. But it wasn't that which made him stumble backwards.

It was the familiar stench now seeping into the cellar.

19

☠ SMELL OF DEATH ☠

'I'm hoping I'm not the only one who can smell that,' said Lazarus turning to Arielle.

'Smell what?' asked Craig.

It wasn't as strong as the reek that had hit him when he'd encountered Red, or the Dead that had taken Clair in the hospital, but it was definitely there on the air, slipping from the space in front of him; of that Lazarus was certain. It was a smell he knew he'd never truly forget, almost as though it had seeped into some dark part of his brain to contaminate it for ever.

The stench of the Dead was in that darkness.

'What are you on about?' asked Craig. 'It's just damp air. And cold.'

Arielle joined Lazarus at the brink of the darkness. She sniffed the air. 'I hate that smell,' she said. 'Always means something bad's about to happen.'

'But why can I smell it and Craig can't? It's just a smell, isn't it?'

'No,' said Arielle, 'it isn't.'

'Just get to the point, please,' Lazarus sighed, frustration in his voice. 'I'm getting tired of figuring stuff out by myself.'

Arielle went back to the desk and leaned against it, her arms folded. 'As I've told you,' she said, 'my role is guardian of the Keeper. There have been many down the years. I protect them. I also bring them into being – and the only way to become one is to experience death and come back. With your father gone to who knows where, I had no choice but to make you a Keeper. And that smell? It's the smell of death. And the Dead ride it.'

Despite what Arielle had just said – and Lazarus knew she'd said it before – it didn't explain what had happened at the beginning of everything for him.

'The smell,' said Lazarus. 'I noticed that when I met Red. Before you shot me.'

'Impossible,' said Arielle, shaking her head. 'You sure it wasn't something else?'

'I checked,' said Lazarus. 'It was definitely Red. And it was there again when Clair opened the rift and one of the Dead grabbed her. It's hardly a smell you forget, is it?'

At this, Arielle's eyes narrowed. 'The only way for a Keeper to be able to smell death is to have died in the first place.'

'I think I'd remember,' said Lazarus sarcastically. 'You're the only person I know who's killed me lately.'

Suddenly Arielle snatched at Lazarus's arm, pulled it towards her, her hand on the scar.

'This,' she whispered. 'Where did you get it?'

'It's just a scar from the car accident,' said Lazarus, wondering why Arielle was so interested. 'Mum died, I didn't. Remember?'

As soon as Lazarus had said those words, they crumbled. He remembered Red, the way he'd reacted when he'd seen the scar, almost like he recognised it.

'You don't think . . .'

Arielle nodded. 'It's the only explanation.'

Craig butted in. 'I'm sure it's all very important, whatever it is you're talking about,' he said, sounding annoyed, 'but it would be more polite to acknowledge that I'm here now and again.'

'I didn't survive the car accident, did I?' said Lazarus, still staring at Arielle. 'The scar ... Red put it there. That's why he recognised it. He ...'

The words stuck in Lazarus's throat. He'd seen Red, spoken to him. So the thought that Red had saved him, now clear as day in his head, was terrifying.

'He what?' asked Craig weakly.

'For some reason,' Arielle said, her voice soft, 'Red saved you, pushed you back into this world. That's his mark on your arm, scorched into your skin.'

'So you didn't need to kill me after all,' said Lazarus. He didn't know whether to laugh or crack Arielle one hard in the face.

'Looks that way,' agreed Arielle. 'Which means you're pretty unique: a Keeper who's died twice!'

'What difference does that make?' said Lazarus.

'I don't know,' said Arielle, frowning. 'And that frightens me a little. Experiencing death gives the Keeper a unique gift to sense the Dead. But this, and what you said happened with that nurse friend of yours ...'

'You're beginning to scare me,' said Lazarus, trying to break a smile.

Arielle turned back to the dark hole in the wall, leaning her head inside and taking a sniff. 'This town has always lived with rumours of tunnels under its streets,' she said over her shoulder. 'Most are dead ends or just little routes between the cellars of large houses and pubs.'

'But nothing like this, right?' Lazarus guessed.

Arielle shrugged. 'Something's down there and we've no choice I'm afraid – we have to find out what it is.'

'You mean we're going down there?' asked Craig. 'Seriously?'

'Lazarus and I are,' said Arielle. 'You're staying here.'

'No way,' said Craig. He looked mutinous. 'Not a chance. You're not going to leave me alone here to wait for some dead thing to come and take over my brain.'

'That's really not quite how I would describe it,' said Arielle. 'And you're staying here, even if I have to nail your feet to the floor.'

Craig folded his arms. 'Well you'd better find a hammer quick,' he said, 'because I'm coming.'

Arielle looked to Lazarus. But Lazarus just said, 'It's his decision.'

A few minutes later, they were standing at the opening, waiting for someone to take the first step. With the aid of the candles and torches they'd found in the house to cut into the thick dark, they could see before them a little more of the worn steps fading down into nothing. They were thick grey flagstones and looked like they belonged more in an old monastery than in the cellar of a house.

The picture Lazarus had in his mind of his dad was now all but obliterated by what he'd learned since he'd opened his bedroom door only a few days ago and smelt that awful smell. New emotions were bubbling up inside him, and he wasn't quite sure how to deal with them. The dad he'd grown up with, he had no interest in, probably just tolerated more than anything. But this dad he'd now discovered was something else entirely. He dealt with stuff that would send most people insane. This was a dad Lazarus suddenly wanted to get to know.

Arielle moved down the first few steps, Lazarus and Craig followed; all of them holding candles and torches to push the dark back. A few steps down, when behind them the door to the cellar was nothing more than a yellow oblong of light, Arielle stopped.

'This goes deep, Lazarus,' she said. 'Tobias was desperate to hide something.'

'Yeah, but what,' said Craig.

'I wish I knew,' said Arielle, and continued down.

It wasn't long before the steps bottomed out into a gravel floor. Lazarus, Craig and Arielle found themselves in a cavern. Their voices echoed in it and the light from their candles only barely managed to reach the roof. It wasn't huge, probably no larger than a village hall, but the darkness seemed even thicker here, thought Lazarus, and it felt like it was trying to grab at their lights and squash them to nothing.

'Where are we?' asked Craig.

Lazarus edged forward, flashing his torch about him. He caught sight of a hole in the far wall and when he went over to investigate found more ancient, worn steps heading down to God knows where. And over by the wall, hidden in shadow, he could make out a pile of long boxes covered in dust and dirt.

'There are more steps over there,' he said, pointing with his torch, 'and some boxes or something. You see anything else?'

Craig and Arielle said nothing.

'The smell is getting stronger,' said Lazarus, turning to Arielle. 'Just so you know.'

Arielle nodded and unsheathed her sword.

'I don't like the look of that,' said Craig, seeing the sword for the first time.

'You're not supposed to,' said Arielle. 'Why don't you two have a quick scout round while I check that exit, OK?'

Lazarus went to walk over to the boxes he'd spotted earlier, but the nausea he was feeling was getting too strong. He needed to sit down.

Craig joined him. 'You OK?'

Lazarus said nothing, but attempted a smile as he lowered himself to the ground. Every other time he'd felt like this, something really bad had happened. He didn't want to even think what was going to be coming at him out of the darkness down here.

'It's a bit weird thinking this is under your house and

you've never known about it, isn't it?' said Craig.

'Dad's got some serious explaining to do when we find him,' said Lazarus and nodded towards the boxes. 'You mind checking those out? Just need to let my head stop spinning.'

'Sure,' said Craig, and headed off across the cavern. But it was when he was nearly upon them that something about the boxes suddenly struck Lazarus as odd.

He called out to Craig, 'Are they what I think they are?'

Craig said nothing and Lazarus watched as he brushed the dust off one of the boxes with his hand.

'There's a brass plaque here,' Craig called back.

'What does it say?'

Craig paused leaned in closer, then said, 'It's just a name and a date: *Richard Harker, 1823–1883.*'

'Coffins,' said Lazarus, his head swimming now, his vision blurred. 'It's a pile of coffins.'

20
☠☠ BLACK SPIT ☠☠

A yell from behind them made Lazarus and Craig whip round. Arielle was falling back from the steps Lazarus had seen in the wall.

'Lazarus! Craig!' Arielle yelled, her sword drawn. 'Get out of here – now!'

Something walked out of the darkness, pulling itself out into the cavern, its fingers scraping against the wall with a sound of nails on a blackboard.

Lazarus saw impossible wings burst from Arielle's back. But where Red's had been ruined and broken, these were utterly, inexplicably perfect. They fluttered in slow motion, thrumming softly in the air, gently lifting Arielle off her feet. The wings shook, shivered, like electricity was charging through them. With a slow, deliberate beat, they lifted Arielle further. She raised her sword.

'Shit,' said Craig.

'Couldn't have put it better myself,' said Lazarus.

He felt a tingle in his skin that took him straight back to the hospital ward and what had happened with Clair. Only this thing now before them made what he'd pulled from Clair look like a child's doll.

The thing was very clearly a man, only this one was closer to a giant. His arms and legs were like the limbs of old trees, thick and knotted and strong, though his skin was pasty white, almost transparent. Over his clothes he wore a stained and burned leather apron that brushed against the floor as he moved. Hanging from the belt around his waist were a number of hammers and the largest pliers Lazarus had ever seen. He looked like a blacksmith, thought Lazarus, and he noticed again how the skin of the Dead shone like it was covered in oil. But, once more, it was the eyes that drew him. And they weren't even looking at Arielle, who was standing right in front of it and screaming; they were staring right at Lazarus and Craig and burned with hunger.

'I said get out!' Arielle yelled again. 'I can deal with this. I can't risk losing you as well as your dad, Lazarus!'

Craig pulled at his friend. 'Come on!' he yelled, unable to drag his eyes away from the monstrous thing trying to push past Arielle. 'Let's do what she says!'

The dead blacksmith swept an enormous arm at Arielle who blocked it with her sword and flew backwards with effortless grace. But her blade was stuck in its arm. She tugged and the blacksmith roared, black spit frothing at its mouth. She tugged again, snapping her sword free, and the blacksmith's arm split, leaking thick blood across the floor.

'Come on, Laz!' pleaded Craig. 'Move it!'

But Lazarus wasn't listening. He was staring at the blacksmith. Something inside him was telling him to approach it; that this was his job and no one else's. Without a glance at Craig, Lazarus moved – towards the Dead.

'What the hell are you doing?' yelled Craig.

Lazarus kept walking. The blacksmith was now trying to swat Arielle like a fly. He roared as he spotted Lazarus, then reached for his belt and pulled out a huge hammer. He swung it at Arielle, catching her right wing and sending her crashing into the roof of the cavern.

Rock and dust filled the air as Arielle yelled and pulled

herself out of the rock. She was too late. Lazarus and the blacksmith were only footsteps away from each other.

Lazarus felt more than a little strange. Deep down he knew he should be screaming, running away, but it was as though that part of his brain had been shut away and all he could hear of it was a faint echo. Even when the blacksmith lumbered towards him, hammer raised, the other arm outstretched to grab him, Lazarus didn't flinch.

The hammer came slamming through the air. Lazarus sensed that what the blacksmith really wanted wasn't to kill him, but to occupy him. And that was impossible if he was squashed flat. So he waited. The hammer skimmed past him and slammed into the ground.

The blacksmith went to grab him. Lazarus dodged easily out of his way. The hand came again, and again Lazarus dodged. Then, when the blacksmith went for him with both hands, Lazarus made his move. He ducked under the huge body as it stumbled and fell towards him, bringing his hands down on to its head with a wet slap.

The skin was slick and greasy. Lazarus felt his fingers sink in deeper than he'd expected, almost like he'd pushed them into soft dough. A screech spewed into the air and the blacksmith shook like he was being electrocuted. Lazarus held on, all the time ignoring that faint distant voice telling him to run like hell.

The screech grew louder. The blacksmith's skin started to bubble and spit. Lazarus knew that even if he tried to, he'd never be able to pull his hands away now, not until this was over.

The blacksmith twisted away from Lazarus, but it was no good; he couldn't get away. Under Lazarus's hands, his skin was smoking and dripping on to the floor like melted wax.

Lazarus was lost to what he was doing. He was totally focused on this creature in front of him. Whatever power he had in him, he could feel it burning in his veins. He wasn't going to let this thing have a chance to escape and taste life again.

Without any summoning, a yell split his own throat and he thrust his hands deeper.

With a final horrifying bellow, the blacksmith bucked and shook under Lazarus's touch. His skin split – and then he was nothing more than a vast spreading pool of steaming slime.

Lazarus stood for a moment, his feet swimming in what was left of the blacksmith. He was aware that someone was coming towards him. No, it was two people. But he couldn't hear them. Then everything went dark.

'Is he OK?'

Lazarus recognised the voice. He opened his eyes to see Craig staring down at him.

'Lazarus?'

Lazarus nodded and tried to sit up.

'Take it easy,' came another voice and Lazarus turned to see Arielle at his side.

'Nice wings,' he said. 'Which reminds me, you never did answer my question and tell me what you are.'

'Take his arm,' said Arielle to Craig, again ignoring Lazarus's question, 'and get him to his feet. He needs to walk around after what he just did, get the blood flowing again.'

Lazarus felt himself pulled upwards. His head swam a little, then the cavern came into focus and he remembered the blacksmith.

'What happened?'

'You carried out more than just an eviction,' said Arielle, and her words just tumbled out. 'You sent one of the Dead back through touch alone. Your Dad, like every Keeper before him, used special chants, equipment, but you used nothing! And not only have you had no training, you did everything instinctively. I've never seen anything like it. In fact, no one has. What were you thinking?'

Lazarus could hear a hint of anger in Arielle's voice, but he ignored it. He felt too tired to argue. 'I wasn't thinking anything,' he said. 'I just saw one of the Dead and next thing I knew I had my hands on it and it was in serious trouble.'

'Is this what happened with the nurse?'

Lazarus nodded. 'I felt more in control this time though,' he said. 'I mean, it was like I actually decided to do it, where as back at the hospital with Clair I was just trying to stay alive.'

'But what was it doing here?' asked Craig shakily. 'And are there more of them just walking around?'

Lazarus shook his head. 'No, I don't think there are any more. I can't smell them anyway.'

'Craig's got a point though,' said Arielle. 'For that thing

to be here at all, it must have got through the veil.'

Lazarus pointed to the opening the giant had emerged from, the one he'd found more steps leading down in to darkness. 'I know we don't want to,' he said, 'but the only way we're going to find out is by going down there.'

'But what about the coffins?' asked Craig. 'Why are they here?'

Lazarus had forgotten all about the coffins. He looked over to where they were piled on top of each other. Seeing them made him feel almost more uneasy than seeing the Dead, though he wasn't sure why. It was as if their presence alone presented a problem, the answer to which no one was going to like.

'The Dead will only use corpses if they've nothing else available,' said Arielle. 'It's a last resort really. They can hide in a living person easily, but a dead person walking around is a little more obvious. People notice.'

'So like I said,' said Craig, 'why are they here? If the Dead aren't interested in bodies, then who is?'

Lazarus didn't like the answer that slipped to the front of his mind like a drunk at a funeral.

21

☠☠☠ CROSSED OVER ☠☠☠

'Dad.'

Lazarus saw disbelief in Craig's eyes. 'You what?'

'Dad brought them here,' he repeated.

'But why would he want coffins?' asked Craig.

Lazarus was thinking back to what they'd found in the workshop in the cellar. Not just the diaries but the notes Arielle had come across. And now the coffins.

'Lazarus,' said Arielle, 'if you've something to say, just say it.'

'I know this is going to sound nuts,' Lazarus began, 'but I think Dad's gone to get Mum. He's the one who's making a hole in the veil.'

Arielle nearly choked. 'Don't be idiotic!'

'I'm not being idiotic!' said Lazarus. 'Don't you see? This

is what it's all been about! Dad's spent years planning it, researching it, and now he's gone and done it. He's gone after Mum.'

'This is not some Greek myth we're dealing with,' spat Arielle.

'I know!' Lazarus said, his voice edging to a shout. 'But it's the only answer that works with any of this!'

'I'm listening,' said Arielle after a moment.

Lazarus tried to explain, but it was difficult, not least because he felt like he was making it up as he went along. 'Red knew someone was trying to push through,' he said. 'He just never expected it to be Dad. Or that Dad had already gone through when he came to see him. That's why Dad's missing. He's not here. He's already crossed over.'

'A Keeper would never consider anything as crazy and wrong as what you're suggesting,' Arielle protested.

Lazarus ignored her. 'There's all the stuff we found in the cellar – his diaries talking about wanting to get Mum back and all those notes about going into the land of the Dead.'

Arielle repeated herself. 'A Keeper would never—'

'Being a Keeper wasn't as important as having Mum back!' shouted Lazarus, cutting Arielle off. 'If you don't believe me, then you go read his diaries, OK? You seem to be forgetting that Dad's just a human. That's it. He lost Mum and it destroyed him and he's spent the rest of his life working out a way to get her back! You said something when we were up in the cellar about needing a good disguise because the Dead would find you quickly. Well that's what Dad's used the coffins for, isn't it?'

'You're not making any sense,' Arielle said stubbornly.

'I'm making more sense than any of this has made since it all started,' snapped Lazarus. 'And I'd bet anything that whatever is in those coffins, whatever's left of the original occupants that they've been stripped of their clothes.'

'But why?' asked Craig. 'What use would that be?'

'It's the perfect disguise,' said Lazarus. 'The clothes of the Dead would have their smell on them. Don't ask me how long it would last, but I'm guessing there's a chance it would be just enough to disguise one of the living and allow someone to walk where only the Dead usually go.'

Arielle walked over to the coffins. She paused, then kicked at one, knocking the lid off and on to the floor.

'Seems you're right,' she said, then bent over and reached inside. When she stood up and turned back to Lazarus and Craig, hanging from her hand was a corpse, its skin not rotten but dried like pork scratchings.

It was naked.

'I really didn't need to see that,' said Craig.

Arielle let the corpse slip from her hand to break on the floor, its skull shattering like a glass bauble. 'If you're right,' she said, 'then your father may well have started something that none of us have the power to stop. Opening a way through the veil is one thing, but to cross over and bring someone back?'

'You look afraid,' said Lazarus.

'I am,' Arielle replied fiercely, 'and with good reason. The land of the Dead is a terrible place – you've seen the kind that occupy it. They're there for a reason. I knew your mum, Lazarus. She would not be there. Her spirit was too pure.'

'I don't care what you think,' said Lazarus, striding off to where the blacksmith had emerged. 'It's the only answer.'

'And that's why I'm so afraid, Lazarus!'

Lazarus stopped in his tracks. Arielle actually sounded scared. And he had a terrible feeling that wasn't a good sign.

'Why?' he asked, looking back at her. 'What's wrong? What's really going on here?'

Arielle's face was still, barely a flicker of emotion showing. But her eyes were alive with a horror that Lazarus knew he didn't want to see. 'Because if it is true, Lazarus,' she said, 'then someone – some*thing* – got to your father and tricked him. It's the only way he'd have considered what you're suggesting. That's what's going on. And that's why we should all be afraid.'

When she next spoke, her voice was dark and hollow and sounded terribly alone.

'The Dead envy the living. What they yearn for, more than anything, is a permanent way through to this world from theirs. They don't have the strength to punch through from their side, but if someone did it from here – if somehow they were able to persuade someone to do it – then there would be no stopping them. The dam would be broken and the Dead would flood out. And you can bet Hell would follow after.'

'Red said the same,' said Lazarus. 'About the Dead envying the living.'

'And he understands better than any of us what that really means,' said Arielle fiercely. 'If you're right, and if your father has gone over, then we have to stop the gap now before it's too late.'

'But what about Dad?' Lazarus protested. 'How's he going to get back if we block the way he got in?'

'He's not, Lazarus,' she said. 'He's lost.'

Lazarus was stunned by Arielle's answer. Lost? Did she mean there was no way Dad would ever get back? There was no way he was ever going to accept that. No way at all.

'We *have* to get him back,' he said, finding it difficult to hold back his anger.

Arielle was striding past him, heading to the dark hole in the cavern wall and the steps no one as yet had explored. 'If we don't stop this now, Lazarus, nothing matters. Don't you understand? The Dead cannot be allowed to return. No one will be safe. It'll be war, Lazarus, or worse!'

Lazarus didn't have chance to respond. Arielle had disappeared into the darkness.

'Now what?' asked Craig, turning to Lazarus.

'I'm not letting her ruin my dad's chances of coming back,' Lazarus answered.

He pushed himself into a sprint across the cavern after her, Craig close behind, and dove down the steps, stumbling as much as running, taking two at a time. They seemed to go on and on, twisting and turning, sometimes in a tight spiral, but Lazarus didn't ease his pace, not even when he bounced in to the wall or nearly tripped. Something was driving him on now and he was letting it pull him on. And with each step, all he could think about was that he was getting closer and closer to his real father. The other one was dead, a shadow behind which the real Dad had hidden all along. He wasn't going to lose him now.

At last the steps came to an end. Lazarus and Craig stumbled out into another cavern. It was about the same size as the one they'd come from but rather than cold and musty it smelled faintly of smoke. Arielle was directly in front of them, facing whatever it was that occupied the centre of this place. When they edged around Arielle, they saw something they could never have imagined or even guessed at.

Arielle didn't look at them. Instead she took a deep draft from her hip flask, then let it drop on the floor, empty.

'What has your father done, Lazarus?'

Lazarus couldn't speak. His voice was trapped inside him and he couldn't rip it out.

'Of all the things I was expecting to see,' said Craig, 'it wasn't that.'

22

☠ LEGION ☠

In the centre of the cavern lay a large circle of burned-out candles. Their sweet charred smell was still in the air. It reminded Lazarus briefly of walking through a cathedral. The last time he'd seen a circle such as this had been with Clair, but then she'd been inside it; not this. Because this was impossible, wasn't it? There was no way it could be here, no way at all.

But it was. After all, he'd seen it in photographs, recognised the people driving it, been told that was him, just there, sitting in the seat in the back.

'It's Mum's,' he said at last, his voice bubbling out of him as tears came to his eyes. 'It's the car she was killed in.'

It was little more than a twisted, rusting shell, a skeleton of the car it had once been, but it was the most haunting and horrific thing Lazarus had ever seen. Red, the Dead, the blacksmith he'd just encountered – none of them had anything on this. His past had stormed into his present. Standing so close to this thing that had destroyed three lives so long ago made Lazarus go cold. Orange rust covered it, and here and there a faint speck of the car's original light-blue paint was visible.

Craig was speechless for a while. He stared at Lazarus and then at the car. 'But how can you be sure?' he said at last. 'It's just a wreck now, doesn't even look like a car.'

'I found some pictures once,' said Lazarus. 'I'd gone into Dad's study. They were on his desk. I never told him I saw them. But they were police photos, I think. Photos of this.'

'Your father must've got hold of it after the investigations into the accident were over,' said Arielle, circling the wreck, her sword now out of its scabbard. 'To get it down here, he would've had to cut it up and rebuild it.'

'Why's it rippling like that?' asked Craig.

Lazarus had noticed that, too. The wreck seemed to warp slightly, like he was looking at something under water or trapped in a bubble, yellow sunlight rippling and bouncing on the surface.

'I found this,' said Arielle, handing something over to Lazarus. 'It's empty because the contents were thrown over the wreck and the candles.'

Lazarus looked at what Arielle had handed him and remembered where he'd last seen it – by the clock above the fire in his dad's office. It was the missing ornament.

'What do you mean by contents?' he asked. 'It's just a vase.'

'It's an urn,' said Arielle. 'The kind generally used to carry the ashes of someone who's been cremated. In this case, I would expect that it contained the ashes of your mother. That was until your dad came down here and threw them all over the place.'

'But what about the rippling?' said Craig. 'Why is it doing that?'

'Dad's opened a way through the veil, hasn't he?' said Lazarus at last, struggling past what Arielle had just told him. How was it that he'd never known the black urn had contained the remains of his mother? 'This car was the last thing Mum was alive in. Dad brought it down here and used it and her ashes to open a rift through the veil. I don't know how, but that's what he did.'

It was almost impossible to take in the amount of work that had gone into not only getting the wrecked car into the cavern, but keeping it secret. But it did go some way to explaining why his dad had always been so distant.

Arielle said, 'The rippling effect you see is the veil itself. That wreck of a car that killed both you and your mum has punched through and is now keeping the hole jammed open. It's how the blacksmith got through. Step through yourself and you'll be walking in the land of the Dead. If we don't close it down soon, more will come. And there will be no stopping them.'

'I'm guessing that's bad,' said Craig, and Lazarus saw him edge away from the wreck.

'We don't know how long this breach in the veil has been open,' said Arielle, raising her sword, 'or if many of the Dead are aware of it. But it won't take long. Rumours spread.'

Lazarus took a step closer to the shimmering veil. 'I hate to say this,' he said, 'but I can smell them. It's only faint, but it's there. They're on their way.'

Craig stepped back further.

'You have to close this down, Lazarus,' said Arielle at once. 'And before you ask, no – I don't know how to do it. I've never seen anything like this before. But you're a Keeper now, like your father. He opened it. You have to close it.'

'I'm not leaving him in there,' Lazarus said. 'What if he's on his way back?'

When Arielle replied, her voice was calm. 'I know this is hard, but you have to understand: we haven't the time! A breach like this will grow and grow until an army could walk through without touching the sides! You have to forget about your father.'

'I can't!' said Lazarus.

The smell in the air grew suddenly stronger. He took a step back. He heard Craig do the same, stumble and fall to the ground.

Arielle looked at him, concern in her eyes, sword still raised. 'Lazarus – I can smell it too. You just need to control your response to it.'

'But it's so difficult,' answered Lazarus, swallowing. 'It's like it's suffocating me.' He took a deep breath, focused, then said, 'I think something's getting close.

It's like when Red came.'

He saw the car shimmer again, only this time it seemed to draw out of focus. Then it was gone altogether.

'The breach is stabilising!' hissed Arielle, her voice desperate. 'Lazarus – you have to close it down! Now!'

Lazarus stared at the space where only moments earlier the car had been. Now all he could see was a silvery blackness in its place, a bubble of thick shadow that pulsed like it had a heartbeat. He felt like he could reach out and touch it.

A screech shot from inside the bubble like the burst of a jet engine, forcing Lazarus and Craig to clamp their hands over their ears.

'Lazarus!' yelled Arielle. 'Do something!'

'But what?' Lazarus shouted back. 'What do I do?'

Another screech; louder, closer . . .

'Anything – follow your instincts! You have to close this before it's too late!'

Lazarus tasted bile at the back of his throat and coughed. He squeezed his eyes shut, pushed the palms of his hands into them, tried to fight the wave of nausea slipping through him. It was overpowering. He bent forward, like he was about to throw up. Then something fell out of the darkness, and he did.

Lazarus wiped the vomit from his mouth, stumbled backwards, knocked into Craig. He could feel himself panicking, losing control, but he couldn't stop himself staring at the thing now pushing itself out of the veil. He'd seen the Dead, how human they looked. But this ... This looked anything but.

It seemed to pull darkness with it in thick, ripped ribbons. It kept oozing through the veil, growing and growing, each movement heavy and deliberate, dragging itself across the cavern's floor with huge, white sinewy arms split with cuts like rifts in a glacier, a slime trail behind it as wide as a river. It squealed and groaned as it moved.

The hands, Lazarus saw, were the size of shovels, and with each pull forward, they would split open and bleed. Of its head, Lazarus could only see a mound of matted hair wet with blood. Its torso was massive and fat like a beached whale, and it was covered in enormous boils that pushed through its skin like they were ready to burst. Lazarus couldn't yet see its legs, wasn't sure he wanted to.

When it was finally through the breach, the thing rested

for a moment, letting out deep, rattling breaths that echoed in the cavern.

Lazarus heard something like bed sheets flapping in the wind. He saw Arielle's wings slip out of her back and lift her gently off the ground as she raised her sword. For a second he felt a sense of hope, that here, facing this thing, they stood a chance. But then the thing's arms tensed and it pushed itself up on to its knees. Arielle was cut off from view. Lazarus gave up all hope.

Oh, God . . .

The boils all burst at once. Bits of flesh flew everywhere. Black and red gore showered and spat from the wounds, drenching the cavern. Lazarus felt the thick, warm liquid cover him, even tasted it. He was unable to look away. From the boils, faces pushed out, all of them twisting and screaming, tugged into impossible shapes. Above them, the creature's head was hidden completely behind the bloody hair that covered it. The faces all turned as one to stare at Lazarus. When they spoke, their voices were a horrible chorus of agony and despair . . .

'We are Legion!'

23
★ HIDEOUS WOUND ★

Lazarus fell on top of Craig who was just sitting, staring at the creature, tears streaking down his face.

'You have to get out of here!' Lazarus screamed, grabbing hold of Craig to shake him. 'Get out now!'

Craig didn't even acknowledge him. Lazarus stood up and tried to pull his friend to his feet, but it was no good. He wasn't going anywhere.

The creature let out a howl. Arielle slammed through the air towards it. The thing swept one of its enormous arms at her and tried to swat her. Arielle ducked, spiralled in the air, then brought her sword down hard. Two fingers split from the hand and fell to the floor. They wriggled around on the ground like giant worms, then bubbled, spat and melted.

The creature howled again, only this time Lazarus heard

a deeper growl behind it, like the sound of rocks falling. It swept again at Arielle. This time it was luckier, and sent her spinning across the cavern and into the rock, which shattered on impact.

Lazarus had no idea what to do. This was nothing like the thing he'd seen in Clair, or the blacksmith. He had no weapons. And he had a feeling that even if he could lay his hands on it, the creature would be too strong for him to have any effect.

He glanced over to Arielle, convinced the impact of hitting the cavern wall would have killed her. He was amazed to see her pull herself out of the rock and brush herself down.

'What the hell is it?' he yelled, pointing at the creature.

He saw Arielle's mouth move in answer, but heard nothing as the creature bellowed and arched its back. Arielle charged, sword swinging murderously. The creature reached out with an arm, but, as it shot towards Arielle, the limb suddenly split in two with the sound of bones snapping and crunching and skin bursting open. From the hideous wound, a snake of bone and sinew and flesh raced out. Arielle dived, but the thing wound round her in an instant and lifted her up, her sword clattering to the floor.

Arielle screamed as Lazarus saw the rope of bones tighten. One of the faces on the creature's body burst from it like a cork from a bottle. Lazarus ducked. The thing flew over his head and landed at Craig's feet. Before Craig could even react, it had flipped over, grinned and pounced on him.

Craig screamed.

Lazarus ran to his friend. When he got there, the thing was nothing more than a slick grey mass spreading over Craig's face and leaking into his mouth. He tried to wipe the stuff off, but it was thick and slippery. No matter what he did, he couldn't dislodge it.

Arielle's voice called out in pain. Lazarus ignored it, his fingers pushed deep into the grey slick, trying to release Craig.

Craig's eyes snapped open. Lazarus felt himself launched across the cavern to land on his back and have the wind thumped out of him.

Lazarus sat up, coughed, tasted blood. Craig was walking towards him, his face pale, his eyes wild. It took Lazarus straight back to how Clair had looked in the hospital. God no ... he realised, *one of the Dead has him ...*

With ferocious speed, Craig ran at Lazarus, his face pulled into an impossible and awful grimace. Lazarus tried to dodge out of the way, but Craig was on him, his fingers round his neck, squeezing hard. Lazarus was choking, saw stars burst in front of his eyes.

'Stop it!' he screamed, digging his fingers into Craig's hands, drawing blood. 'You're strangling me!'

He tried to push away, kicked his heels into the ground to get some purchase, pulled at Craig's hands. Nothing was working. He could feel his head starting to spin.

A shout from Arielle made him turn.

'Evict the Dead inside him!' she yelled, pain in every word as she struggled in the creature's grip. 'Now! Before it's too late!'

But Lazarus didn't have the strength. Craig's hands were winning and he could feel himself losing consciousness. It would be easy now, he thought, to just give up.

Something clattered to Lazarus's side. He opened his eyes, twisted his head. He could see Arielle fighting against the creature. Her wings look tattered and broken, but she'd managed to get one arm free and was pointing at the thing that had landed next to Lazarus – the spike he'd used in the hospital. But hadn't he left it in Arielle's truck? She must have brought it with her, he realised.

'Do it, Lazarus! NOW!'

Lazarus looked back up into Craig's face. It was twisted into a snarl, eyes sunken and black. He wasn't going to let the dead bastard take his friend . . .

With a yell that felt like it would rip open his rib cage, Lazarus brought his hands up to Craig's head, clamping it firmly between them. When they touched he felt a jolt like electricity. Craig let out a shriek that could've shattered glass. Now Lazarus could see the thing inside him. It snarled and tried to pull Craig free, but Lazarus wasn't letting go – couldn't even if he'd tried.

The Dead made Craig attack Lazarus with everything he had, biting and scratching and thumping him. Lazarus felt Craig's teeth sink into his arm, was caught in the face by a left hook, but still he couldn't let go. The more the thing made Craig attack, the more determined Lazarus became. He pulled himself up to his feet, dragging Craig with him, until he was face-to-face with his friend. Then he swung him round and slammed him into the cavern wall. Craig's body convulsed, his mouth opened and a black torrent of slurry burst out on to the floor. Lazarus felt him go limp.

Allowing his friend to slump to the floor, Lazarus stood back and bent down for the spike, his eyes on the unconscious Craig. He knew this wasn't over yet. As he expected, and just like it had happened with Clair, something started to push from Craig's body, hands and head first. When it was fully out, Lazarus stood over it, calm and cold.

'We are many!' it sneered, dragging its pallid body towards Lazarus.

Lazarus cocked his head to one side.

'Now you're one less,' he said, and, dropping to his knees, brought the spike down, right through the thing's head. It didn't even get a chance to squeal.

Lazarus heard Arielle fall to the ground as Legion shook in pain and anger. Pulling the spike from what was left of the Dead that he'd evicted from Craig, he watched her push herself to her knees and look over at him. She was in a bad state, her wings tattered and torn, her face bruised and bloodied.

'You must close the veil, Lazarus,' she coughed, rising to one knee and reaching for her sword. 'I'll deal with Legion. You aren't strong enough, not for this.'

'But what is it?' asked Lazarus, glancing back at Legion, gripping the spike hard in his hand. 'How can it be one of the Dead? I thought they were human souls – nothing like this!'

Arielle rose to her feet. 'Some demons consume souls, Lazarus,' she said. 'They feed on their energy.'

'Demons?' said Lazarus. 'But I thought—'

Arielle cut him off. 'Forget what you think! Just understand that Legion did not come from the land of the Dead. It came from somewhere much, much worse – Hell!'

Lazarus went to reply but saw Legion coming before Arielle did. The thick rope of bones and blood caught her across the side of her head. She slammed into the ground and was still. The rope came again, grabbing at Lazarus. He dodged it, dodged it again, then swiped at it with the spike. Legion screamed. When it came again with the rope, it went instead for Craig.

'No!' yelled Lazarus as his friend, now almost conscious, was lifted high into the air.

The thing paid no heed. Craig was whirled around until, with a throw that snapped the rope of blood and bones in two, Lazarus's friend was sent silently, helplessly through the veil.

24
INTO THE RIFT

Staring at where Craig had disappeared, Lazarus was unable to comprehend what had just happened. Now not only had he lost his dad, but his best friend too. He wanted to yell and shout and scream, but he knew it would do no good. Never did.

Lazarus turned from the veil to face Legion. He was gripping the spike so hard that the metal thorns on the handle bit through the cloth wrapped around it, piercing his skin. He could feel the warmth of his own blood flowing between his fingers to slide down the spike's blade and drip on to the floor. But he felt no pain.

He took a step towards Legion. Every face on its awful torso laughed, their mouths black, their eyes like dead pools of stagnant water. With each step, the monstrous thing laughed louder and louder.

A movement to his left made Lazarus turn. Arielle had uncrumpled herself. She looked worse than ever. Blood was gathering in pools around her.

'Not on your own, Lazarus,' she said, trying to stand. 'You're not strong enough. Not for something like this.'

Another voice joined in. Lazarus turned to find every single face in Legion's body was still, eyes closed. Except for one. A woman. She smiled darkly at Lazarus and started to push out from among the rest.

Lazarus stared as first the head, then the shoulders, emerged. When the woman was free to her waist, she simply slipped out and landed on the floor in a pool of dark slime. For a moment she didn't move, just lay there breathing. Then, slowly, she got to her feet.

Lazarus stared at her. How normal she looked. She was slim and tall and black hair ran down her back. She was wearing jeans and a T-shirt, but Lazarus thought how she looked like she'd just taken a bath fully clothed; everything was sopping, and liquid dripped into pools on the floor as she walked forward.

Lazarus stumbled back, just out of reach of her two pale hands, unable to take in what he was seeing.

It can't be ... It just can't be ...

Arielle, now on her feet, limped across the cavern, her wings dragging behind her. 'It's not what you think, Lazarus! Don't believe what you're seeing! It's trying to trick you!'

The woman smiled. Lazarus felt what was left of his world collapse around him.

Mum ...

He took another step back, but a rock on the floor caught his heel and he tripped and fell to the ground.

'You're not my mum,' he cried, scrabbling backwards as the dead woman drew nearer. 'You're not her!'

But it was. He recognised her, not from memory but from all the photos of her around the house.

The woman smiled. 'I miss you,' she said, and opened her arms like she was reaching out to hug him.

Lazarus could feel tears coursing down his face. It couldn't be his mum, could it? What if it was? What if she'd been trapped inside that thing called Legion and was now free?

He tried to move again, but felt his back thump into the cavern wall.

'I miss you,' the woman said again, only this time Lazarus saw her eyes widen horribly, like they were stretching.

A shout from Arielle slapped Lazarus hard.

'Duck!'

He had just enough time to register the blade of the sword zipping through the air before he flattened himself on the floor. Arielle had thrown it from where she stood.

The woman screamed, her right arm cut clean through by Arielle's sword. It spun across the cavern. When it landed on the floor, it flapped like a freshly caught fish and started to steam and dissolve.

The woman snarled and pounced towards Arielle, who leapt backwards. Lazarus took the chance to get himself to his feet.

'It's not your mum, Lazarus!' shouted Arielle, as the woman faced her. 'It's feeding off your emotions to get you to see what it wants you to see!'

'But how do you know that?' Lazarus replied, his voice breaking. 'How can you be sure?'

The woman turned back to Lazarus. He could see the stump where her arm had been. There was a deep cut in her side where Arielle's blade had made contact. She stared at him, her face blank. Then a black grin slipped across her face. With ferocious speed she sprang across the cavern towards him.

Lazarus had nowhere to go – the cavern wall was behind him. He raised his arms to protect himself. The impact of the woman knocked him to the floor and he cracked his head hard. He tried to push her off, but something wasn't right; she was stuck to him somehow, unable to get off.

The spike ...

Lazarus glanced down to see the spike still clasped in his hand. The rest of it was buried deep inside the woman. She screamed and thrashed against the metal, her face twisting and contorting, but it did no good; she couldn't pull away. Lazarus kicked her off. She flipped on to her back and the spike stayed where it had thrust, deep into her chest. Her hands were on it and she was pulling at it and thrashing, but nothing she did could shift it. Deep splits grew either side of the wound, spreading across her body as it fell apart in great steaming chunks. Then the spike slipped further in, disappearing completely, and what was left of the woman popped like a bag of pus.

Lazarus stared at what was left of the woman. He reached down and picked up the spike. For some reason, he realised, the spike was capable of destroying the Dead. He didn't know why, but that didn't matter for now. Not with what he was about to do next.

Lazarus snapped round and hurled the spike at Legion. He heard Arielle gasp, but that was the only sound in the cavern as the terrible piece of metal sped through the air, then hit its target. The spike sank into Legion completely, piercing an eye of one of the faces covering its torso.

For a second, all the faces were still, shock etched into each of them, their mouths open in fear. Then they all screamed. The sound only ended when, from the place where the spike had entered, Legion's body was suddenly riven by deep bloody gullies.

'Lazarus!' shouted Arielle. 'Get down!'

The explosion lifted Lazarus off his feet and sent him spinning through the air to land next to Arielle. For a few seconds, he could hear bits of what had been Legion landing around them, wet and reeking.

'You OK?'

Lazarus sat up and nodded.

'That was . . .'

'No kidding,' said Lazarus.

He stood up, walked over to where Legion had been standing, and in a pile of what looked and smelled like rotting meat, found the spike. He pulled it free, then headed towards where he'd seen Craig disappear through the veil.

'You can't go through there,' said Arielle, her voice strained as she lifted herself from the floor and stretched out her wings. 'You have to close it. Now.'

'My best friend and my dad are on the other side,' Lazarus replied.

'But if you don't shut it now,' said Arielle, 'Legion will be like a picnic compared to what will soon follow. Red has failed, Lazarus. Hell has broken free.'

'I can't leave them,' said Lazarus. 'You know that, don't you?'

Arielle picked up her sword. 'You have to close the rift, Lazarus!'

Lazarus smiled. 'I know,' he said.

And then, before he had a chance to change his mind, he dashed up the steps to the room in which he'd fought the blacksmith. When he returned a few minutes later, Arielle saw what he was carrying and stepped in front of him, resting her hand on his chest.

'Don't do this, Lazarus.'

Lazarus held up what he'd brought down from the room above – rags of clothes he'd found in the other coffins. 'If it worked for Dad, there's a chance it'll work for me and Craig.'

'You don't know that,' said Arielle.

But Lazarus wasn't listening. He slipped into the torn, dirty, stale clothes: an old jacket with ripped sleeves and trousers that had once been smart but were now musty and spotted with mould. He then walked towards the rift.

'Lazarus!' Arielle called. 'Don't do it!'

'You know,' said Lazarus, pausing briefly, 'you never did answer my question.'

'Which one?'

'What are you?'

'Aren't the wings enough of a hint?'

Lazarus shrugged, raised an eyebrow. 'Funny way for an angel to make a living.'

'The pension's good,' said Arielle.

Then, before he had a chance to change his mind, or Arielle could stop him, Lazarus stepped into the rift.

And as the darkness swallowed him, the last thing he heard was Arielle yelling his name.

The adventure continues in
Book 2 of THE DEAD:

THE DARK

Coming soon in October 2010

Turn the page for a sneak peak . . .

THE DARK

The creature could smell blood and flesh. And it wanted to burrow itself into it, like a worm into an apple, set up home and live again.

The creature had only faint memories of what it was to be alive. But that had been a long, long time ago. So long that the memories were no longer images, simply sensations; like phantom pain after an amputation. Yet it could remember the things it had lusted for. It made it breathless to even think about them.

What it had been, man or woman, old or young, it had no idea at all. It could summon up a faint recollection of pain around its neck, but nothing more than that. The pain had no connection to anything else, no picture, no image. It had tried to work out what this pain meant. Perhaps it had been hanged? Beheaded even? But it had never discovered anything deep inside, no clue. Nothing. And it had changed so much over the years into something so far beyond what it had looked like or been, that even a reflection would not have given enough of a clue.

But its basic instincts hadn't changed. Or its tastes. And that drove it forward tasting the air, sniffing it. It knew only the thirst that could not be quenched: the thirst for *life*. Blood was pulling it forward. It would find the body that it coursed through, slip into it and *live*!

It just had to get to it before anyone – *anything* – else did . . .

As it shuffled and scuffled forward, it couldn't shift a dull notion of confusion. How could the smell of blood even be here in this place? Everything was dead, fresh blood did not belong. Perhaps it was a gust from the other side? New arrivals of fresh-faced Dead, often brought with them the faintest of smells of the living. But that always faded so quickly. Yet this . . . well, it wasn't fading at all . . .

The house was cracked and broken; black brick and stone and shattered glass, like a building after the Blitz. But the creature wasn't concerned; everything looked like that here. And it slipped forwards, glided up the path to the remains of a front door. There was no garden; just dead earth and dust, dried and split like sunburned mud. Or scorched, blackened skin.

With a glance back to the street to check it wasn't being followed, the creature eased itself through the door; it looked like a gaping mouth of sharp, broken teeth, the thick wood planks split and charred. The hallway swept round past a door on the left leading to a room at the front of the house and to a staircase that pulled itself up to the first floor on a rotten, crumbling banister, for ever caught in its last moment before total collapse. A death freeze.

The creature paused here for a moment. Something in this place was not right. It could smell the body stronger now than before, almost hear its heart beat, and it was coming from further on and below the house. A cellar perhaps? This was no wisp of life from the other side. It was a body — of that it was sure. And it was here. In the land of the Dead. Someone had been past this way before, and very recently. Someone *alive*. Someone *walking*. A body was strange enough, but a living person actually walking in this place? Surely it was mistaken . . .

The creature ignored the nagging thoughts and confusion. It turned to its right, away from facing the stairs. In front of it was another door, swinging uselessly on one hinge, fading carpet split with mould on the floor just visible in the gloom beyond. The hallway turned left, along the side of the stairs and on to a room with an upturned table and chairs, all broken, with smashed crockery littering the floor. But the smell wasn't coming from there. It was coming from an opening under the stairs that led down into a darkness that was dry and heavy.

The creature slid into the black. It would get to the body and no other would know about it. It anticipated the moment when it would push itself into the flesh, force its tongue to loll from its mouth, to drool an oily slick on to the floor.

The darkness gave way to a room with smashed shelves and desks, all covered with the dusty remains of clocks. A corner of the room reeked of rancid wine and the creature glanced to see a mound of broken bottles. The far wall, opposite to where it had entered, contained an opening and steps faded downwards. It followed them, came out in another cavern with a gravel floor. This was an empty place, but for the crumbled remains of a few coffins. In the far wall lay another opening. The creature almost skipped to it with excitement and down to where it led.

Here it was! Yes, this was it!

The creature stood still for a second, allowed itself to adjust to where it was. It was in another cavern, larger than the last. This one was lit strangely and at its centre it could see something mangled and wrecked, a mess of twisted metal. It had no idea what it was or could have been before it had been destroyed. But whatever it was, it shimmered a little, like it was on the other side of a pool of water.

The creature then heard breathing; the sweet sound of one of the living just footsteps away. It turned and saw the body lying against the wall of the cavern, covered in rubble and dust. It looked young, male. It looked . . . perfect.

It turned to the body, leaned down so close that it would taste the boy's breath, then opened its black mouth. In a few moments the creature would seep into it, take it over completely, and the whole thing would be a delicious ecstasy.

Then something fell through the shimmering light around the wreck of metal at the centre of the cavern. And when the creature saw what it was it almost screamed with delight.

ABOUT THE AUTHOR

DAVID GATWARD

Previous job: Salmon Farmer
Loves: Horror movies
Hates: DIY
Fact: Seen two ghosts

David was born in Bristol and grew up with his two younger brothers between the Cotswolds, Wensleydale and Lincolnshire. Aside from having a huge number of hobbies including: caving, camping, climbing, archery, shooting and music, David also wrote avidly. Although he had his first book published aged 18, it's taken many more years and life experiences to lead to writing *The Dead*. Seeing two ghosts, being mistaken for a homeless person and almost drowning have given David plenty of food for thought, but it's his family who've been a big inspiration. Now living in rural Somerset with his wife and two boys, David writes full-time and hopes to see ghost number three very shortly.

Questions and Answers with David Gatward

What do you enjoy most about writing a book?

You're playing God! Seriously – you're immersed in a world that you created, running around with characters you dreamt up, battling evil ... and winning! When you realise the story is working, that the characters are as real as they could get, you find the story just starts racing ahead and you have to keep up. It's strangely exciting, a bit weird and scary, and completely enthralling. I cannot express how lucky I am to be in a position to be writing books. It's astonishing.

What do you least like about writing a book?

The fear of knowing you've got to come up with a story can be terrifying – the fear of the blank page/screen. Those days when nothing happens in your head, when it takes hours and hours and hours to come up with just a few hundred words, and each one of them really, really hurt. Deadlines approaching too fast. The fear of failure haunting you with each book you write, that it'll be total junk and the world will laugh at you and force you to wear pants on your head for the rest of your life.

Writing seems to be a very solitary occupation – are you someone who's comfortable with his own company?

Yes. But that doesn't mean I'm a hermit in a cave with a crab as my only mate. Writers need solitude to get on with it. But I've trained myself to find that anywhere (I wrote a book on train journeys over a period of five weeks). I write with the world blocked out, but when I'm not writing I love being around the people that make my life fizz and buzz and thump.

What was your favourite book as a child?

The one which sticks with me is *The Weirdstone of Brisingamen*, by Alan Garner. It has this one bit in it, where the heroes end up crawling through a water-filled tunnel and they have no choice but to go through it, not knowing if they'll get out or drown. It still haunts me today!

Have you ever seen a ghost?

Yes, I have seen a ghost. Well two, actually. The first, a man dressed all in black, appeared one sunny morning while I was mowing a lawn. Didn't say much; just stared. Kind of freaked me out though. The second, a woman in a blue dress, woke me up in the middle of the night while I was living in a caravan (which, just so you know, was situated on what was once an old graveyard). Pretty weird, particularly as, despite it being dark out, inside, the caravan was all lit up.

Who are your heroes?

I don't have any in the conventional sense, but I do have a few people I admire. These include (in no specific order): my dad, an old friend Michael Forster, and writers Linda Chapman and Neil Gaiman.

What do you do in your spare time?

As I'm making the transition from full-time yawn-filled job, to full-time 'WOW!' writing, I don't really have spare time! But in the bits I find, I hang out with family/friends, read, listen to music, cook ... and try to work out if I'll ever have time again to do stuff like play the drums, go climbing, go to the gym ...

What's your guilty pleasure?

Glee!

What's your dream car?

Landrover Defender 110 King Cab (done out to my own spec, obviously).

If you were a superhero, what would your power be?

The ability to fly. That sense of freedom, to be able to just take off and zip through the sky ... I'd so totally love that.

What is your perfect sandwich?

Er ... well, this is the one I have late at night: peanut butter, mayonnaise, Danish blue cheese, sliced onion, and cheese and onion crisps. Yeah, I know ...

ANTHONY
HOROWITZ
HORROR

Collection of horror stories by No 1 bestselling
author Anthony Horowitz.

It's a world where everything seems pretty normal.
But the weird, the sinister and the truly terrifying are
lurking just out of sight. Like an ordinary-looking
camera with evil powers, a bus ride home that turns
into your worst nightmare and a mysterious
computer game that nobody would play...
if they knew the rules!

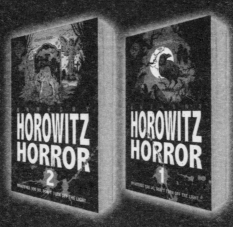

ORCHARD BOOKS
www.orchardbooks.co.uk